Strange Faces

Linda Hall

Published by the author as a member of the
Alexandria Publishing Group

Strange Faces

ISBN – 978-0-9877613-5-4
ISBN – eVersion: 978-0-9877613-4-7
Formatting by RikHall.com
Cover by BookGraphics.net

Contents

Pickers and Choosers

I blame you Desi, for my crap life. You are responsible for this job which has me on my feet eight hours a day serving martinis to droolers who come in here thinking that gives them the right to ogle me. I blame you, Desi, for the nightmares—that girl's face pressed against the windshield, her mouth opened in a scream. I heard her then. I hear her now. Every night of my life. I blame you, Desi, for my bum knee which hurts like hell when it rains. Like today. My scar from that night. My wound which will not heal.

It rained on that night, too. The night we killed that girl. No. I will amend that. The night you killed that girl.

You're up there on the television now with your white-teeth smile, your politician promises, all those fancy ties of yours. No sports on yet here in the bar, so instead we've got the news on, muted but with the captioning picking its way across the bottom of the screen like little white crabs. What's with you always wearing a tie?

Twenty-seven years ago you killed a girl. You would deny it, of course. I can picture you holding up your fingers. "Number one," you would say, "It wasn't a real girl. Number two, you were hallucinating, and," with a flourish of your third finger. "If someone did die out there, all of us are equally to blame. We were all drunk." Then you would laugh.

We weren't drunk. Not me. In those days I didn't drink much or even do drugs. That didn't come until later. Etta didn't either. When I think back I honestly don't remember her ever raising the paper cup of brandy to her lips. I do, though, remember the way you led her roughly by the elbow back to the truck arguing with her while she tried to break away. "There is no dead girl!" You yelled. "You will remember that for the rest of your life. There is no dead girl!"

I didn't go to the police that night. My knee was too screwed up to walk. By the time I was ready to limp around again, you were gone. All of us were gone. It was like our little group of trash pickers— you and Etta and Boyd and Caroline and Angel—had never existed.

It's too late to report you now. I can't go waltzing into the police station after twenty seven years, can I, and put my fist down on the counter and say, "I'm here to report a murder?" No. No one would believe me and that's my fault. I've made it so people don't believe me. Look at me. Bum knee. Can't quit the smokes. Live alone in a one room box of an apartment that leaks. Crap job. Look at you, Desi. Big Man. Rich. Lots of lawyers I bet, too.

I should have insisted on driving on that rainy and awful night. No matter how you laughed at me, I shouldn't have let you drive. When you said something, anything, we, all of us, went along. I, who had come late to the group, was the only one who every once in a while tried to defy you. It didn't work then. It probably wouldn't now.

A part of me died on that road and despite years of looking, I never found out who we killed that night. That frightens me still, like when you hear the wind at night in the high, dark branches of the trees.

I saw her face. I was in the passenger seat when she bounced over the front of the truck and landed for an instant against the windshield, mouth opened, eyes wide. For months after it happened I expected the police to come. I waited for them, even. I vowed I would tell them everything. They never came. After all this time and they never came.

There you are, up on the television on this black and miserable afternoon, with your big shiny face grin, the way you talk as if you can smooth everything over like syrup on toast. I have kept tabs, Desi. I know about the deaths of your first two wives. The first one, barely a year married before she died in a car accident. Not your fault. Of course not. And then marriage number two. She died too, but not until you'd been married for seventeen years. Cancer. At least that's what they're saying. I have my doubts. I think a lot about poison while I mix drinks night after night behind this bar. I read that you're onto trophy wife number three. Ellen Somebody.

I kept track of you through the years, Desi. I have watched your rise to fame, first becoming the best-selling real estate agent in the whole city (oh wow, cool you), and then running for various political offices. Always in the news. Always drawing attention to yourself. It's like you're thumbing your nose at everything and everyone. Like you're daring Etta or me to come after you.

Back then we didn't have the Internet or Facebook or anything so it was a lot more difficult to find people. It's easier now. You're everywhere—Facebook, Google, even Youtube. You've got this stupid little real estate video on how to "stage" your house for "showing." What? Really? Are you friggin' kidding me? When you grin into the camera it's like you're laughing at me, daring me, showing me how far you've come. How you can get away with anything.

I pick up a wine glass and polish it. I check on the beer stores. Mid-afternoon and it's pretty empty. It'll fill up once Happy-Hour-Half-Price-Wings starts at four. But for now it's you and me.

I'm about to reach for the remote to turn you off, when a dreadlocked kid comes to the counter and asks for a coffee. People wanting coffee at a bar always surprises me. Everyone knows that bars aren't known for their coffee. I guess I'm leaning a bit wrong because when I pour him his coffee, I wince a little.

"You okay?"

I look up. "Old war injury."

"Know the feeling." There's this look of sadness on his face as he sits there and quickly downs his coffee. After he's gone I wonder about him. I was about his age when it happened.

Two days after the girl died, I got up and made myself stumble down to the corner pay phone. I needed to talk to Angel. If anyone in our group would know how to get ahold of Etta, it would be Angel. I called the place Angel was staying, but no one knew who she was. This was the number she'd given me. Strange.

Next, I tried Boyd. After he helped me get home and bandaged my leg, he'd written down his number on a piece of paper and left it on my table. "In case it's bad in the morning, I'll take you to the hospital."

No answer there either. It would be different now with everyone having cell phones. We'd all keep in touch throughout the week, maybe even get together for a brew or a joint now and then. It wouldn't just be one night a week.

I've often wondered through the years whether you got to them first. I wouldn't be surprised if by now they're all dead. It's only a mercy that you didn't know where I lived. I was always pretty secretive about that. When you started driving me home, I got off a good three blocks from where I was staying. This was mostly because I was embarrassed by my one room in a corner of the basement of this known crack house. The people who owned the place let me stay there, rent free, if I didn't bother anyone. I kept my word. I kept to myself. Sometimes I gave them food we found, so that put me in their good books. The only one who saw my place was Boyd on that night when he half-walked, half-carried me home.

It wasn't until two weeks later that I was able to limp enough to take the bus back to the alley where we'd hit her. I wasn't surprised that there was no sign of anything having happened. By this time there weren't even any scuff marks on the road. You would have taken care of that.

I ran into Boyd only once after that. A dozen years ago I was in SuperFoods, the same one with the dumpster out back. Why I went in there, I have no idea. Maybe it was the same reason Boyd did. I was picking up a bag of chips, and there on the other side of the aisle was Boyd. I froze. It felt like all the blood from my body had fallen through my veins and landed at my feet. I was cold all over and hot in the next second. Even though the years had added to his face I knew him immediately and know he recognized me. His eyebrows shot up and he started to make toward me. I gasped, dropped the chips and leaving my half-filled grocery cart right in the middle of the store, I ran outside. I've never been back there. Not once.

Seeing Boyd like that, it was suddenly that night and I was screaming at him, "Get Desi to turn around! Boyd, we have to go back!" My eyes were wet with tears, my face flushed and frantic as I grabbed for you, for Boyd. Someone do something! Do something! Something!

Boyd couldn't. Nobody could make you turn around if you didn't want to.

Thursday night was our night. It was the night our little band of dumpster divers met at the dumpsters in the strip mall behind the SuperFoods. We were young. We were idealistic. We were saving the world and this was the ultimate in recycling, wasn't it? It was amazing the things we found— loaves of bread hardly a day old, dented cans of veggies and fruit, yogurts only a day or two expired, cartons and boxes of milk. After we gathered up all of our treasures, it was you who decided how everything would be divvied up. What I took home became my food for the week. Some I gave to my landlord. Some I traded for smokes.

Speaking of cigarettes, I sure could use one now. My fingers are shaking as I look up at your face on the TV. Next to you and in the shadows is your new wife. I wonder how long she'll last on this planet before you get rid of her.

The camera pans her briefly. I put down the wine glass I am polishing and grasp at my throat. *What*? I am absolutely still. It can't be. Maybe I'm mistaken. I have to be mistaken. I look more closely. The woman is Etta! I read that her name was Ellen, not Etta. Yet that is Etta.

I remember back then, the darting of her eyes which made her look perpetually fearful, the pale hair, long and wild then, curly all over. Now, it's sleek against her chin, highlighted by the looks of it. And her eyes, those same smoky, dark eyes. Always obedient to your every command, she was.

Except that one time.

And now she is *with* you? I look carefully. Is it my imagination or does she flinch away from you, ever so slightly when you touch her? No one else would see this. I do.

Yes. I have thought about blackmail. At night when I can't sleep, when I see that girl's face up so close to mine, I work out elaborate plans. I never carry them out. Is that why you married Etta? Did she threaten to blackmail you? Did she finally rise up and try to defy you? You, of course, would end up with the upper hand. That must be what happened.

Even Boyd knew what you were. Before he left my room that night he had taken my face in his hands and said, "Marie, leave it alone."

I was new to the group. I was the outsider. My joining was quite by accident, and he was warning me. I don't even know how long the five of you had been together before I became a part of it. As I stand here watching you and Etta, I am back there at the very beginning of everything.

At that time, I was supplementing my meagre existence with food and clothing from various dumpsters in and around the city. It's amazing what you can scrounge, and I was good at it. Full jars of pickles, packages of hamburger meat, barely bruised heads of lettuce, hardly brown apples. Even chocolate and baked goods. And then there were the clothes, lots of clothes and shoes.

I did this by myself and nobody bothered me. I didn't know then that there was this hierarchy of dumpster divers, a whole subculture of pickers and choosers, groups with their own nights and their own dumpsters and their own carefully managed times.

I'd been knee deep in my favorite dumpster when you and the others showed up. My found items were lined up on the ledge of the dumpster—an expired jar of sauerkraut, a bag of not too soft carrots, some taco shells, a loaf of oatmeal raisin bread—only blue on one side, a couple packages of white chocolate, and a pork chop, still in plastic.

I was rooting through a plastic bag which looked promising when I heard your truck pull up, stop and then voices. I covered myself in cardboard and hunkered in a corner. The last thing I needed was for the police to come or someone from SuperFoods to cart me away. I had no idea if what I was doing was illegal or not. I stayed that way for a long time, praying that no one would notice all of my scroungings. You did of course.

A girl's voice, the girl I would come to know as Angel yelled, "Hey, look at all this stuff. All here."

"Someone's been here." It was Boyd who said this.

"Lettuce!" came another voice.

"Our work's done." It was you, Desi, who said this. "Or mostly."

You were kids just like me, and dumpster divers, and I wasn't about to give up an evening's dirty work. I stood up and said, "Those things are mine."

You looked me straight in the eye when you said, "You're wrong there. Those things are ours. This is our dumpster and this is our night."

This was my first introduction to the unwritten code of the dumpster divers. I mumbled, "It's a free country."

"No, it ain't," the girl I would come to know as Caroline said.

I saw Etta then. She was leaning against the hood of the truck. Her face was so pale it looked like a moon in the dark night. When I glanced her way, she turned away from me. In our eight months together she and I barely spoke. That she would ultimately stick up for me in the end was flabbergasting.

I said to the group, "Who says? I've been coming here a long time. This is my stuff, you idiots!"

At that point in my young life I had a very acute sense of fairness. As I've gotten older I realize that nothing about living on this planet is fair. Nothing at all.

Caroline shot me a warning look. I ignored her.

"Cool it," you said. "We can work this out."

As far as I was concerned there was nothing to "work out." I began climbing out of the dumpster. "I'll just get my things and get out of here then. How 'bout I do just that?"

You came and stood in front of me, your face

inches from mine. I have to say it now—you had presence. Back then you had presence, what some might call charisma. The fact that you were kind of good looking didn't hurt. Plus, at that point I thought you were a normal person.

You said, "You seem to have the knack for finding things. You will join us."

It was not a question. It was a statement. You touched the end of my nose with your finger, an odd gesture, a far too intimate gesture, and I flinched away,

"Coffee grounds," you said. "On your nose."

I brushed furiously at my face.

I climbed back into the dumpster and the chubby girl, the one called Angel, got in with me. Together we worked, laying the stuff on the rim while the others wiped things clean and put things in piles. Angel quietly told me how everything worked. You were the leader of this group, she said, and we were "lucky" to have this series of dumpsters. The series of dumpsters was the best in the city. I already knew that. I learned that Etta was your girlfriend.

"Sort of," Angel added. "That part's not really clear. Sometimes it seems they hate each other. They have a history. Don't know what all it is, but they have this history."

The loner part of me was pleased that they wanted to include me. It made me feel a part of something important. At the end of that night, you divvied up our findings. I went home that night with more food and goodies than I had had in a long time. Maybe this would be a good thing. I came back the following week at nine and we did the same thing.

After a month you offered to drive me home. I

got up onto the bed of the truck with the others and climbed under the tarp so we wouldn't be stopped by the cops. Etta always sat in the passenger seat with you. That's why I wondered why I was up front on the night it happened. In the years that followed, I've wondered if you planned it all. Me in the front to witness the accident, Etta in the back. I've had a lot of time to think about things.

I continue to stare up at the television, at Etta, at her sleek hair, at the trim blue suit on her impossibly thin frame, at her attempt to smile for the cameras. I look at her and I am there, back on the night it happened.

On that Thursday night a sleety gray rain was blowing sideways and I was soaked and cold before we even got started. Winter was coming. I was going to need gloves. Didn't have any. I didn't know what we would be doing once winter hit. Would we still come out every Thursday night? We didn't talk about this and I didn't ask.

Whether by design or accident for eight months now, I'd always been the first to arrive. I liked being there first. It gave me an edge, I thought. Tonight they were all there ahead of me, standing outside of the dumpster arguing with each other. I knew what about. It's what we always argued about, whose turn was it to actually go into the dumpster. Usually it was me. I didn't mind. I was dressed for it tonight in rubber boots and dirty clothes that I saved special for Thursday nights.

"I'll go in," I said. "I'm wet already from walking."

Being on the inside had both advantages and disadvantages. Disadvantages because you were the one who got really filthy. Dumpsters are not filled with nice neat unopened packages of food. There's a lot of slime and fish heads and just plain grime, even dog shit and vomit. The advantages were you could slip small things into your pockets undetected—chocolate bars, little packs of M&Ms. These were favorites of mine that I hid away from everyone and never shared. I think we all did this.

I climbed up onto a box and over the edge where I fell into into the dumpster, my hands grasping the nearest thing which was an edge of a cardboard box. The container was really full that night. You pointed to Caroline. She shrugged but of course, she did as she was told. I was a bit disappointed and wondered at the changed order of things. Usually me and Angel were a team. Boyd normally worked with Caroline, and you with Etta. I really liked being with Angel. She told me things about you. About Etta. About all of the members of our group. I don't know if half the things she said were true, but I loved her stories. Sometimes it was about life in general—growing up with five sisters, how she got married once for a month to a lunatic. Me, who'd never had much in the way of family, hung onto her every word.

The whole back end of the dumpster was full of produce that night, head after head of iceberg lettuce. Trouble was lettuce and broccoli weren't exactly our favorites. Even though in those days we all pretended we were "save the planet" vegetarians, we pretty much preferred chips or candy and cans of soup. One by one, we handed the lettuce heads to Boyd and Angel. Etta, I noticed, was sitting on a wooden box underneath the grocery store overhang where out of the rain, she placed our pickings into piles.

Wedged behind a couple of boards I came across the ultimate prize–two unopened bottles of wine! This was rare! This was a find!

"Hey!" I called. "Look what I got!"

Behind the wine were two more bottles of whiskey. "Wow!" I yelled. I passed them out to Boyd, who called you over. You decided that these would be for us. When we finished for the night we would celebrate.

As the years have passed, I have wondered if this too, was part of your plan. Did you put those bottles there ahead of time? Did you plan for everyone to get drunk that night?

Caroline took this discovery to be a good omen. She kept saying, "This is gonna be a great night!"

"Yep," I said. I don't know why, but it felt just the opposite to me.

I was pulling up one of the last heads of lettuce when Caroline began screaming. She scrambled breathless to the front of the dumpster where she grasped the edges, frantic, breathless, yelling, crying, shaking all over.

"Caroline," I said. "What?"

"A body!" She pointed. "Back there. A person. And her hair fell off!"

"What!"

"I'm not going back there. I'm getting the hell out of here." She barely needed anyone to help her clamber out, but Boyd caught her nonetheless.

I looked back and saw where she was pointing. Nestled down between the greenery of rusted lettuce leaves, dirty bits of kleenex, candy wrappers, muffin crumbs and coffee grounds was a perfectly round face. Eyes opened. Pink skin. High cheekbones, small red mouth, black wig askew on a bald head. I felt my stomach lurch.

Everyone was talking at once. Caroline wanted to leave immediately. Etta already had climbed into the back of the truck bed and was pulling the tarp over top of her. Angel, in typical Angel fashion went over to the dumpster, hiked herself up and looked inside.

"We're not going anywhere." It was, of course, you who said this.

Despite our protests, you calmly walked over and climbed into the dumpster. A moment later you were dragging that dead girl's body to the side of the container. You lifted her bald head over the rim with one hand, and with the other you held up a black wig.

You said, "Is this what has you guys so afraid?"

I hung back, looked away. I was sincerely trying not to throw up.

Caroline groaned.

"It's fake!" you yelled. "It's a store mannequin, you friggin' morons!"

You placed the black wig on the doll and arranged it on her head. Angel was the first to venture forward and place a tentative hand on the doll's plastic hand.

"He's right. It's not real."

I stared and stared at the thing. It had straight black hair, chin length, and eyes which were faintly Asian but sort of not. The skin on its face was pale as porcelain. The mouth full, pouty and bright red, was skewed up at one side in a bit of a smirk, like she was having us all on. She reminded me in that instant of you.

"Boyd," you said, "Help me sit her up here on the edge."

You smoothed its hair and Boyd helped you set the unclothed mannequin on the edge of the dumpster. It was like having a seventh person there, watching us. I wanted her to be back in the dumpster and all covered up.

The fact that she was naked seemed to bother all of us. On the ground next to the dumpster was an old laceless running shoe, rubber half gone. Angel put it on her right foot. It was too big. She tied it tight. Even Etta got into the act and brought over a ripped piece of tarp from the truck and draped it it artfully around the dirty thing, trying it at her waist with a piece of twine. I was surprised that Etta did this. Angel whispered to me that Etta was an art major. As if that explained things. You grabbed a couple of lettuce leaves to make a bit of a hat for her and Caroline placed an empty coffee cup in the thing's hand, arranging it so that it wouldn't fall out of the stiff, inert fingers.

By the time Caroline and I were back in the dumpster unearthing treasures, the doll thing was perched on the corner of the dumpster, clothed in bits and pieces of detritus and holding a paper cup and watching us.

All of us were strangely quiet that night. It was like there was a pall over the entire group. Or maybe it was a harbinger of things to come. I didn't want to look at her.

An hour later you told us that we were finished for the night, but not quite. Laughing, you opened the wine. You went and got a wine opener from your truck. Did you always carry one in your glove compartment? Something else I have wondered about in all the years that followed.

You opened the booze and we shared it around.

I was too keyed up to drink much of it. The rest of our group drank from paper cups we found in the dumpster which were sort of clean. Underneath that drizzly sky, we sat around on the ground or on boxes while the dumpster lady looked down at us from her perch. Something we never did on dumpster nights was to drink.

You even gave her a name, Rosie.

"Hey Rosie, you want some of this?" You poured brandy into the cup she held. It lodged precariously between plastic fingers.

Angel said, "Hey! Don't waste it on her!" She grabbed it and drank down the paper cup like a shot. By the end of the night there seemed to be more empties scattered about than what we had found. Did you bring extras? Was that part of your elaborate set up? A fish and loaves sort of miracle?

In the years following, I have looked for Rosie. I found websites where stores buy display mannequins. I have never seen her face. I found online places where guys can buy full sized girlfriend dolls with names like Bianca and Tiffany. I scrutinized their faces. Every one. Rosie was not there. When I pass a store front I always look at the mannequins. Rosie is never one of them.

When we were ready to leave, when the last of the liquor had been consumed, the wind came up and so did the rain. Rosie fell hard to the ground in a puddle of muck, her hand still in that outstretched position. Her empty cup went flying.

"Let's go," you said. "Let's get out of here."

"We can't just leave her like that," I said. I have no idea why I said this.

"Then go get her and throw her back in the dumpster where she belongs." Your voice had an edge to it that frightened me.

I walked over to her intending to do that. I can't, to this day explain it, but I couldn't make myself touch her. It was like she was looking at me with those half-Asian eyes. Maybe it was a trick of the rain encrusted street lights, but I could swear that her eyes followed me. And something else. Behind those eyes, she looked frightened. Like somebody was really in there and wanting to get out.

I swallowed and backed away to the truck where the rest of the group were loading our treasures. I don't remember too much of what we brought home that night. By the time Boyd had half-carried me into my room and dressed the wound in my knee, I didn't care.

Etta was up in the truck bed and shivering and packing her own food treasures into her backpack. I made to climb up onto the bed, but you grabbed my arm. "Ride in the passenger seat."

"Me?" I looked at him unsure, and he nodded. I climbed up into the cab, wondering but grateful to be out of the rain, while the rest of the group crawled underneath the tarp in the back.

"Are you okay to drive?" I asked. Your speech was a bit slurry.

You laughed at me without answering. Up there in the cab I felt uneasy around you as I always did. Still laughing, you put the key in the ignition.

It happened quickly and without warning. One minute I was thinking about being home and dry and wondering if the main floor bathroom would be free for a shower, and in the next a girl with straight black hair to her chin and bits of tarp tied around her waist with string, and carrying a paper cup in an outstretched hand was limping toward us down the middle of the road. Limping because she wore only one shoe, an old running shoe that looked too big for her.

I screamed. You were heading straight for her, seeming not even to see her. I lunged for the steering wheel to get us out of the way. The truck veered, but not in time.

I felt the thump more than heard it, and then for a brief second her face pressed against my side of the windshield, before she fell away and onto the road. But I remember the way her eyebrows arched up, the slight tilt to her eyes, her lettuce encrusted hair, the coffee grounds on her cheeks. Instead of the smirky full lipped smile, hers was a mouth with real human lips and she was screaming.

"Desi!" I screamed and pointed, "That was— that was—." I couldn't say it.

You swerved wildly to the left. I looked back and there she was, still on the side of the road. Moving? Still alive? Maybe. It looked that way.

"That girl!" I yelled reaching for your arm. "You hit her! We have to stop! We have to go back!"

You got the truck back on a straight course and without missing a beat you said, "What girl?"

"The girl! Look." I pointed to the smear of blood on the windshield. It stayed just a minute before the next round of rain washed it away. "She's hurt. The girl. We have to go back."

You slowed down a bit and turned to me. "How much did you have to drink, Marie?"

"She was—. Didn't you see her? The mannequin girl." It made no sense.

"The what?" You were full on laughing now. It was a laugh that I had to get away from, a laugh that frightened me so much that I opened the passenger door and without thinking jumped out. I fell onto my knee in a bout of pain which enveloped my entire body. But two things I knew—you had hit someone, and I needed to get away.

You stopped the truck with a jolt, and demanded that I get back in. But I couldn't move. By this time I could hear the others in the back talking and clamouring down from the truck bed.

"Did you see her?" I kept asking the group over and over.

"See who?" Caroline asked.

"What's the matter? What happened?" Angel asked.

"The girl," I managed to say. "The mannequin. We hit her. She's back there. On the road." My words were coming out in short bursts between the gasps of pain as I lay on the ground.

"The mannequin?" Angel said. "What are you talking about?"

I heard you say, "Marie thinks we hit a zombie."

Boyd came over. I kept shaking my head. Over and over. Trying to explain what I know I saw. "She's just back there. Go check. Right back there."

Boyd was touching my face and shushing me. I was surprised at how gentle he was, and how knowledgeable he seemed to be when he knelt in front of me and pulled up my pant leg and placed warm hands around my leg, feeling here and there.

"I don't think you broke anything," he said.

I kept protesting. "We have to go back." And then in the next moment I nearly passed out from the pain. Boyd helped me up a bit, but I could put no weight on my leg. I groaned and turned in time to see Etta running back down the road.

"Come back!" You were yelling at her, but she

was running. Running faster now. Running away? I don't remember too much, because by this time Boyd had helped me into the cab of the truck, my knee bleeding profusely. I leaned my head onto the back of the seat trying to quell a rising nausea. Boyd ripped the sleeve off his own shirt and wrapped it around my knee. "I'll take you into your place. Then we'll have a better look." Quietly he said to me, "My mother's a nurse. I know a bit about things like this."

I was surprised at this. None of us talked about family much. It was as if we had all arrived out of the ether.

I dimly remember your loud voice. I had never heard you quite that angry. I half-turned to where you had grabbed Etta by the elbow and were steering her back while she was biting, hitting, yelling to get away.

"There's no one back there!" You were yelling. "Do you understand! No one. We hit no one." You slapped her face. Hard. "Do you understand me? We did not hit anyone."

"But I saw," Etta was shouting. "It was that doll. Des, I saw! You won't get away this time. Who was she? Why did you kill her?"

It registered only briefly that I needed to talk with Etta. I would find her. If not tonight, then tomorrow. Some other time. But I never did.

Our group never met again.

Over the next few days I kept scanning at the news, sneaking looks at the television news, but there was no mention of hit and runs. I began to wonder if I had imagined it. Sometimes I still do. Or if it was some sort of ghost. Or something. But Etta saw it, too. And that makes me know that it was something real.

And now as I stand here, massaging my knee, I am thinking. You are with Etta now? Why are you introducing her to the world as Ellen? But I know. I don't know how you managed it, but I know. It *was* something real.

Seeing Etta today convinces me Rosie was real and you had somehow set up the whole thing. You wanted to kill that girl, so you found a mannequin and made sure we all dressed her up like that girl. It was you who brought the alcohol. You came up with an elaborate plan and you carried it out. Somehow you did it all. Why? I have no idea.

In that quiet bar, I remember the other things about your life, the hidden things that I have found by patient searching. I kept a record of all of them. I wrote everything down, the mysterious death of your wives, of course. And then there was that assistant of yours, the one who fell in front of a moving subway train. Suicide, the papers said. Funny that. Etta is next. I know this. I am sure of this.

I hang the rag by the sink, write a quick note to my boss, grab my jacket and walk the four blocks to the police station. I put my fist down on the desk and say, "I'm here to report a murder."

Strange Faces

A Nice Cup of Something Hot

I was sitting in the backseat of a police car, a grey wool blanket around my shoulders sipping hot coffee from a Styrofoam cup. The snow had turned to a kind of sleet, which on the roof of the car sounded like cutlery dropping. I was sitting there because I had just killed someone. That's what they do when you kill someone, they give you coffee and a grey blanket and sit you in the back of a police car.

In the storm, my car had skidded into a drunk who'd staggered onto the road. There was nothing I could do. At least that's what I told the police officers who came and found me crouched over him, my own good wool coat sopping up his blood and covering his neck, which had bent at that awful angle.

Shock does strange things to you. It makes you cold when it's warm and warm when it's cold. I sat beside him in the road, in just a cotton sweater and jeans and hadn't felt the cold until later. Until now.

I had told my story at least two dozen times. I hadn't seen him. I needed a few things at the drugstore, and yes, I had gone out on a night like this. I hadn't realized the streets were quite this bad until I was around the block from my apartment, and no, I didn't think to go back. I should have but hadn't. I was halfway to the mini-mall by the time I realized how deep the snow was, how awful the roads were. That's what I told them. They wanted to know what I'd bought. Band-Aids, extra strength Tylenol, Nice 'N Easy Dark Ash Blonde and Nail Slicks nail polish in Perle #820. I showed them the bag. They didn't look inside.

If you're wondering if I was being honest with them here, I wasn't. Shoppers Drug Mart hadn't been my primary destination. Well, yes, I'd been in there. I bought all those things that I said I bought, but that wasn't until later. What I'd really needed was scrapbook supplies. I'm a mad scrapbooker, totally hooked since taking a "Preserving Your Memories" workshop at the Needles 'N Trims store. They close at nine, and I needed supplies, so I'd gone out. I'm so hooked that when I want string or ribbons or sparkles, I want them now, if you know what I mean. It was only later that I thought about nail polish, and once inside Shoppers, I remembered my grey roots and my headaches.

Since my husband left me, walked out of a perfectly good thirty-one year marriage and began shacking up with his bimbo, I've been trying to do things for me; scrapbooking, colouring my hair, looking nice, making the effort.

The front door of the police car opened, bringing in the snow and wind. A new face peered back at me, this one belonging to a cop, so young and peach-faced that he looked like Spanky of Our Gang. I'm talking about the television program, not the music group. I remember them both. When I was little, I was always half in love with Alfalfa. The young cop climbed in and shut the door. He smelled like snow, and I had the urge to touch his jacket, feel the cold on him.

"Mrs. Wilkers? Is there anything you need? Is there anybody I can call? A family member perhaps?" His voice was so gentle that my eyes watered.

I shook my head. "No. I have no family members. Not since—" My voice trailed off. Why had I started with that?

He bent his head at me, nodding, urging me to go on.

"I'm—I'm divorced." A fresh batch of tears. He reached back and patted my shoulder. He seemed so kind.

"They're going to have to take your car for a little while," he was saying. "They need to have a good look at it. I'll be driving you home in the SUV." He was still patting my shoulder awkwardly, like he was unused to such ministrations.

And I was weeping again, shaking my head and weeping. He handed me a Kleenex, and I blew my nose. I wonder if some scientist somewhere has ever measured tears. How much can a person cry before there's no moisture remaining in the body, and it dries to a fine white powder and blows away like sand? I had pretty well not stopped crying since Hal had walked out on me.

"You ready to go home, or do you want to sit some more?" He asked.

"I'd like to go home now."

He came around, got me out, and led me gently, his hand on my arm. "The SUV is better for this weather."

I climbed into the SUV. "I forgot my things," I said. "Can I get my things out of my car before we go?"

"Certainly. I'll get them for you."

"The Shoppers bag on the front seat and my purse."

He left, and through the frosted windows I watched him approach the huddle of the police and the ambulance drivers. They were moving the body now, lights flashing through the snow.

Of course, I'd been crazy to come out in the storm. Hal always called me crazy. Said he couldn't live with a crazy woman anymore— Crazy, crazy. My entire body was trembling. I closed my eyes and pressed my lips together to keep my teeth from clacking against each other.

"You didn't tell us you went to Needles 'N Trims," the young cop said to me accusingly when he climbed into the SUV. I stared at him, open mouthed. He was smiling. Okay, it was a joke after all, and I saw what had happened. The bag from Needles 'N Trims had somehow fallen out of the Shoppers Drug Mart bag. He handed both to me.

I quickly put my Needles 'N Trims back inside the one from Shoppers, rolled the top of it down and didn't say anything. My scrapbooks were my private affair. My things. My time for myself.

"Do you do crafts?" He asked, pulling out onto the snowy road. "My mother does needlepoint," he added.

I looked out the window. The ambulance was driving away, slowly, sadly. No need for hurry, no need for sirens now. The lights looked blue against the snow. The dead man was Ernest Rodhever, Ernie to his friends. Bank manager and member of the Rotary. Recently divorced from Rebecca Rodhever. He would probably have a big funeral full of words from kith and comrade. The victim was unknown to me.

"I have a picture in my kitchen she did," he was saying. It's of a wagon train in snow. Like tonight. Only instead of a car it's a wagon train. Framed. You'll have to direct me to your house."

"Down this road a mile or so. At the light, turn left onto Brisbane. It's the Westminster Apartments. I'm on the fifth floor."

"The Westminster apartments?" He turned to look at me.

"Yes."

A few minutes later he said, "Quite a commotion there a few months back."

I shrugged. I knew what he was talking about. Everyone who lived anywhere near Westminster apartments knew that Bruce Searshot had fallen to his death off his fourth floor deck. Some said it was suicide. Others thought it was an accident. The findings by the police were inconclusive.

Outside, the sleet had changed to a kind of half-rain that sounded like hands patting on the top of the vehicle. He asked me if I knew the man who'd fallen, and I nodded and said I knew him to see him, that was all.

When we stopped at a light, I asked him his name. He adjusted the mirror and said, "I thought I told you. I'm sorry if I didn't. I meant to. It's Robert. Call me Rob."

"Isn't that interesting. My son's name is Rob. He's a stockbroker. Investments. Bay street."

"Perhaps I could call him for you."

I looked down at my hands, the veins like thick worms crawling across my flesh. When had my hands gotten like this? When had I become this woman with hands like this? I used to be so young. There was a time I was even pretty. "No. Don't call him."

The air in the car was stifling. The young always make it too hot for us. They think we like it that way. I placed the back of one hand against the window, trying to extract coolness from the pane.

Ahead of us, the lights of a twenty-four-hour coffee shop on the corner from my apartment looked surreal through the snow, like a painting on the calendar.

"Would you like a cup of coffee?" He asked.

"What?"

"We could stop for coffee. I think we both need to unwind a bit. Have a cup of something hot."

"That would be nice."

He parked in front of the coffee shop, and he came around to take my elbow as he helped me down from the SUV, as if I was an old woman. Well, maybe I am. Maybe to him I am. And then I thought how nice it would be to have a son who did this, a son who walked his mother into a coffee shop at eleven at night to get her a nice cup of something hot to drink.

There were a few other patrons in there. Two men were at the counter talking about the storm, and a young couple sat together in the far booth and held hands across the table. There was a time, years ago when that could have been Hal and me.

He ordered coffee, and I asked just for a cup of hot water, please. I don't often drink coffee, and certainly nothing with caffeine this late at night. I'd had a couple of sips of coffee in the police car earlier and would probably pay for it later.

Rob was pleasant and talkative. I mostly listened while he told me about his wife and baby at home, about the new house they were building across the river, about how his wife wanted to do the bedroom in a kind of yellow and how he wanted blue. I told him how lucky he was to find love. After a few minutes he said, "Tell me about your divorce. It must've been very painful for you."

I looked down at my cup. They'd given me a teacup instead of a mug. That was nice of them. "It was very hard."

He looked so serious, so intent, the way he touched my arm, like no son had ever touched my arm, so I told him my sad, sad story.

Later in my apartment, I couldn't sleep. You'd think if I just killed someone, that's what would've kept me awake, but no, it wasn't that. It was all that talking about Hal. He shouldn't have left me. It just wasn't right. It wasn't fair. I fell into tears again. Hal. Hal.

I cried as I dumped out my new scrapbooking supplies onto the kitchen table. I had two days worth of newspapers to go through. I cried as I plugged in my kettle. I wept as I went through my papers and added pictures and addresses. I sobbed when I pasted them in, adding colored strings and ribbons.

At around six in the morning, I fell into a restless sleep. In my dream, I was running my car over Hal and his bimbo, the way I'd run over Ernie. Only in my dream I kept running over them, back and forth, back and forth. Then I dreamed that Hal was falling, turning over and over as he fell to his death from the deck. Instead of Bruce Searshot falling the way he did, it was Hal, and it was me who had pushed him.

The ringing telephone jarred me awake.

"Mrs. Wilkers?" I sat up on the couch where I'd slept.

"Yes?"

All over me were paste and markers and newspaper cuttings and scraps and scrapbooks. I had left the cap off the red marker, and through the course of my turning and tossing, I had written an elongated Z on the couch cushion. There was also some red on my forearm and a bit on my face.

"Mrs. Wilkers, this is Rob."

I cleared my throat. "Hello."

"I was wondering how you are."

"I'm okay."

"You sure?" He sounded so caring, so son-like. "It was quite an ordeal you went through last night."

"Thank you for calling, Rob."

A few minutes later, I got up and went to the bathroom. I really wanted a bath, a nice bubble one, with candles even, but a sponge bath would have to do. I've been bathing this way for six months now, filling the sink with water, leaning my head into it to wash my hair and then sponging off the rest of me.

Behind the closed shower curtain was a heap of bloody clothes, encrusted and dried to a dark brown by now. I couldn't go in there. I couldn't even move them to a safer place.

Before I washed my hair, I carefully removed the red from my cheek with dabs of cold cream and cotton balls. I'd have to be more careful. I'd have to pay more attention.

In the kitchen, I boiled more water, poured

myself some Kashi and got out my scrapbooks. The little matter of the red Z on the couch worried me. I hoped the couch wasn't ruined. If I couldn't fix it, it would be yet another thing in my apartment that would be off-limits to me; like my bathtub, my computer case, and the 21.7 cubic foot freezer that I kept in my second bedroom. The whole second bedroom would soon be off-limits to me.

I drank hot water from my tea cup and wandered through the day's newspapers, which had come through the mail slot. I get four each day, two in the morning, one in the early afternoon in one at night. I managed to find six more pictures of Hal. These I cut out.

You may wonder that I can find so many pictures of my ex-husband. Well, Hal's a real estate broker, so his picture's in the paper, plus on a lot of lawn signs, like he's running for office. When he first left me, I'd taken from driving from house to house late at night, parking behind bushes, venturing out and defacing his picture with black magic marker. I drew on moustaches and beards and put round circles around his face with lines through. I thought I was quite clever. No one would suspect me. How could they? A respectable woman-of-a-certain age writing four letter words on For Sale signs? Think about it.

I'd also managed to find a picture or two of Maura. That's his mistress. It's always a little more difficult to get pictures of her, and sometimes I have to resort to taking them myself. Sometimes I follow her, keeping well behind as she does some ordinary task like grocery shopping, and there I am at the ready with my digital camera. Then I put them on my computer and print them off.

I stacked my scrapbooks on the coffee table. I put Hal's scrapbook on top of Maura's, then I got out my murder weapons one.

I collect murder weapons. Well, I don't really collect the actual weapons, I don't want you to think that, but what I collect are pictures of murder weapons used in actual cases. I follow trials—I sometimes even go to them—and when the murder weapon is mentioned, I look through all my books and magazines for pictures. I've been pretty lucky in finding just about everything I've needed. I've got pictures of guns, knives, pillows (These are easy to find – just go to any Sears ad in any newspaper and you're bound to find pillows!). I've found fireplace pokers and cast-iron frying pans in ads for Canadian Tire, but my all time favorite has to be a curling trophy. Yes, someone actually killed someone with a curling trophy! It took me a while to find it, but I lucked out when a rink in our town had some sort of a bonspiel, and there was this picture of the skip holding up a trophy right there on the front page of the sports section!

Sun glinted through my window. I got up and closed the blinds. The snow was deep, but at least it had stopped. Down below, Clyde Frodiff was shovelling, and across the way, old Mrs. Gibb was sweeping off her deck. That woman, always sweeping snow, never shovelling, always sweeping. I hope when I'm that old I don't get like that. I looked down to the place where Bruce Searshot had fallen off his deck and onto the ground. Being one floor above him, I knew exactly where the place was. If I squinted, I could almost see him lying there still.

The intercom buzzed. I pressed "talk", thinking it might be the mailman or the courier guy.

"Mrs. Wilkers? It's me, Rob."

I buzzed him up, and while he was on the elevator I scrambled to shove my scrapbooks under the couch. Then I closed the doors to my bedroom and the bathroom attached to it. Then I turned on the television as if I'd been watching it all along. Old women watch television, and in his estimation, I would probably fit that bill.

"Would you like some tea?" I asked him cheerfully when he came to the door. "I have the kettle on."

"I would, thank you."

I knew he was just being polite. Police officers don't usually drink tea. I know this, but on the other hand, I don't keep coffee around. Hal used to drink coffee, but when he left he took with him all the remaining canisters of Tim Hortons along with the Mr. Coffee.

"Are you here with news about my car?" I asked.

"Not yet. I'll keep you posted on that." He stepped into my kitchen, stood there looking around. "I just have a couple more questions for you."

While he talked, I looked at the apartment through his eyes and saw the trashcan heaped with paper cuttings, my newspapers stacked in a corner of the living room floor, the scissors, my bottles of glue, my marking pens, bits of cloth, ribbons and colored string. I also saw the dishes in the sink, a loaf of bread on the counter, the cereal box, the butter where I'd left it, the dirty knives on the sideboard. Back when it was Hal and me, I never would've stood for this. I used to have a girl who came in and cleaned for me once a week. I don't have her anymore. Sometimes I regret not having her anymore.

The kettle whistled, and I unplugged it got down the teabags. I'm very fond of Earl Grey.

"It's about your ex-husband, Hal Wilkers," he said.

I turned suddenly, almost pouring boiling water on my hands. "Hal?"

"You told me he left you. I got the impression from you that it was fairly recently, and that's why you weren't yourself last night." His cheeks were flushing purple. "But my information says it's been five years. He's remarried and they have a child."

"He went and married someone young enough to be his daughter!" I sloshed water onto my counter, that's how much my hands shook. "What kind of a man goes and marry someone half his age? How do you think that makes me feel? And a child!" I managed to still my fingers enough to get two tea bags in the pot and pour water over them. I set the works on the table with the cozy on top.

"You also said you had a son name Rob. I looked that up, too. You have no children, Mrs. Wilkers. You and Hal had no children."

"He has a child with that Maura!" I spat out the words. I was shaking now, like last night. "I was mixed up last night. I've been through a lot. I may have said strange things. I don't even know what I said!"

I turned away from him to the sink, pulled off a paper towel from the roll and dabbed at my eyes.

He was holding a bottle of glue, turning it over and over in his hands, looking around, not saying anything. It was making me nervous. Then he sat down at the kitchen table, poured himself a cup of tea and started drinking it, still not saying anything. I asked what colour he and his wife had decided on for their bedroom. Anything to change the subject. He told me yellow. That's a good choice, I said, but he kept looking at me. Finally he asked that if I didn't mind, could he check in on me periodically? His own mother was gone, and he felt a kind of responsibility toward me. Still trembling, still shaking, I said that was fine. Before he left, he asked to use the bathroom. I said okay and led them to the half-bath off the hallway.

He hugged me before he left. Hugged me! Then he said he was sorry. He knew I'd been through an ordeal, he should have been more understanding about Hal.

When the afternoon paper came, I boiled the kettle again and began skimming through the divorce section. Oh, I know what you're thinking, there's no such thing as a divorce section like there are for births and obituaries. But really there is, if you know where to look, and I do. It's the auction section, the legals, those little notices absolving a man—it's always a man—of any encumbrances and debts owing against him. I found a few. Also, I looked for trials and murder weapons to add to my collections.

I found more pictures of Hal. I used my scissors and cut his nose and placed it in one ear, and put his two ears where his eyes should be, and cut out his mouth and placed it upside down. I laughed at that, and you would too, if you seen what I done to him! I wonder how it would be if I did that for real?

Rob called me the next day, and the next day. And the next. I got my car back at the end of the week, and still he called. Usually he ended up talking about his baby, who was changing every day, he said. He promised to bring me pictures the next time he came over. He always asked how I was doing. No one had ever done that, not even during those early days when Hal left. On Tuesday he called to tell me that this little girl had a new tooth, her first. She was standing, too, well, not on her own, but walking along furniture, that kind of standing. I said how nice.

On Saturday, a full two weeks after it happened, Rob called again. "Just tying up some loose ends, Mrs. Wilkers, just trying to get a handle on things." He cleared his throat. "A man in your church, Thomas Gillian, died of food poisoning a year ago at a church supper? Do you remember that, Mrs. Wilkers?"

"Well, of course I remember that! I quit going there after that! Something like that happens in the church, you just lose your trust in people."

"Hmm," was all he said.

A day later, he called and asked about Marta, my cleaning lady.

"I had to let her go."

"Her family reported her missing six months ago."

I said, "The day she disappeared, she confided in me that she planned to run away to Vancouver. I told the police as much at the time."

But I have to say that his questions were making me nervous. Why was he asking all these questions, especially when he was so nice to me? Most people aren't, you know. Your husband leaves you, they automatically think something's wrong with you!

When Rob didn't call for four days, I looked up

his name in the phone book. I didn't find it. Well, lots of police officers have unlisted numbers. You can't be too careful these days, especially when you have a wife and a baby daughter to think about. So, I called the police station and was told by some secretary, probably, that Rob was out on a call.

"Poor thing. He works so hard, and especially with his wife and baby at home. I just wanted to invite him in for supper."

There was a silence, then, "Wife and baby?"

"He promised to show me pictures next time."

More laughter. "You sure you are talking about Rob? Our Rob? That guys as single as they come. In fact he's more single than they come. He's the party animal to beat party animals. Wife and baby!" And then she laughed some more.

I hung up. All day I worked on my scrapbooks. Didn't eat lunch. Had no supper. No tea. Worked feverishly. I knew what was going on. I didn't just fall off the turnip wagon, not me. I knew the price of tea in China. He was getting like Marta. Steps would have to be taken.

Two days later, he called. "Mrs. Wilkers? I'm sorry I didn't call you. I was away for a few days with Mandy and the baby."

"Oh?" I kept my voice steady, cheerful. Mandy and the baby! "I would love it if you and your wife and baby could come for supper, Rob. That would please me very much. You've been so kind to me."

He told me that his wife and daughter was spending a few days at her mother's, but he'd love to come by himself. Fine, I said, just fine.

The following day he was standing at my door, and I was offering him a nice cup of something hot to chase away the winter cold.

"I have a few more questions for you," he said taking a sip and pronouncing a good. "About that man who fell off the deck here. It turns out he'd left his wife about a month before he died. Did you know that?"

"Hmm," I said, drinking my water and watching him sip tea.

"Also, the man who died in your church, he'd left his wife, too."

"There's a lot of that going around. Men leaving their wives for younger women."

He looked at me curiously. "How do you know they were younger? I never told you they were younger."

I shrugged. "Only a guess."

I'd made my green bean casserole, you know the one—with the frozen green beans and the dried onions rings and cream of mushroom soup. But since I can't use my freezer anymore, I had to rely on canned, so it wouldn't be as good, probably. But, it would be highly unlikely that we get that far. I'd end up eating that stuff for days and days. He kept drinking his tea and looking at me. Looking. Looking.

After I put him in the freezer, and that was no small feat with the big guy like him, let me tell you, I boiled the kettle and had myself a cup of Earl Grey.

I'd thrown Rob's rings into my computer case, which had become the receptacle for such things. I thought about my coat then, my good one that I'd used on Ernie Rodhever. I wondered if I would ever get it back. Well, if I did, I'd add it to the others in the bathtub.

Later on, after I put plastic wrap on the rest of the casserole, I pulled out another scrapbook from underneath the couch, the one on serial killers. My favorite. I'm especially interested in female serial killers. There aren't many, you know. Well, there is that one they made a movie about. Did you see that one? I think she got an Oscar. Maybe someday someone will make a movie about me. Maybe she'll get an Oscar, whoever they get to play me.

Strange Faces

We Are Brothers

Red-faced, scowling and without a word, my brother stumbles through the back door and scrambles to get past me and down to the basement where he lives. I lean my kitchen chair back on its hind legs, but despite his considerable bulk, he manages to arch past me so that we don't touch. My brother doesn't like touching. When people touch him he howls. Sometimes this goes on for a long time.

"Hey," I say. I was drinking my coffee and watching the news. I'm starting on afternoons and kind of getting myself geared up for a week of not seeing Shelley much. Shelley, my wife teaches kindergarten.

"How's it goin'?" I say, trying to keep my voice light. I always try to keep my voice as light as I can when dealing with my brother.

He doesn't answer me. The only sound is his labored breathing, worse today. He's big, huge, and getting fatter by the day. I worry for him, his heart in particular, but of course there's nothing I can do about it. We're both adults and he can live the way he likes. Shelley keeps telling me this. My brother doesn't look at me today. This is not unusual.

What is unusual is the time of day. Shortly after noon and he should be down at the car wash until he gets off at four. Has he been fired from yet another job? I sigh.

Then I see something which sends a chill through me. He's carrying a humongous knife, like a butcher knife. Blood drips down the fingers which clutch the knife. Drops trickle onto the floor. When he sees my opened mouth, he quickly shoves the knife under his belt. He says nothing to me. I return my chair down to its four legs. Hard. My coffee spills.

He pauses on the top step and pants hard through his mouth. In. Out. In. Out. He wipes his bloody hand on his jeans. I wait.

He says, "If someone comes—"

I make fists with both hands. I know my brother's rages. I know how he can absolutely snap if touched the wrong way, if touched in any way at all, really. I'm just about the only person who can touch him, and I have to make sure he's in a good mood. I'm the one who always ends up going with him to every doctor or dentist appointment.

"If someone comes?" I can barely speak.

"I—I just want to go home—. Tell them. Tell them that. If someone comes. I want to go home. Home."

I stare at him. He wants to go *home*? What does he think this place is for him? He's been living here at my house, mooching our food for the past six months, getting us—me, really— - to cover for his every failing. If this isn't home, I don't know what is.

I look at him, at his red bulgy face which is breaking all out again. I wonder if he's still taking his prescription.

He's shaking his head. "—I had nothing to do with it." His voice has taken on a whiny quality. "It wasn't my fault."

"Fault about what?" I can barely get the words out.

"People shouldn't make fun of other people."

Very carefully I formulate the words. "Was someone making fun of you?"

He nods slowly up and down.

"Is that the story of the knife?"

Another nod.

I get up. "Hey, you want some coffee? We can talk about it." A thin slice of fear is tracing a path down my spine.

He is making his way down the stairs. "Home," he says over and over. "I want to go home."

I follow him down. I try to talk to him. I try to urge him to tell me what happened, and that everything will be okay, if he just trusts me. I'll take care of it for him. Like I always do.

He goes into his room, and the first thing he does is sit down at his humongous computer screen and wiggle his hand on the mouse, bringing his world alive. He removes the knife from his pants pocket and without looking at it, places it beside him on the desk. He pays so little attention to it it might as well be a set of keys he has laid there. The blade end is covered in blood.

I am desperate now to get him to talk before he becomes immersed in his game. When he gets into his medieval war game his regular day to day life fades from his thinking.

On days when the two of us have been able to have a rational conversation, (not today!) he has told me he considers this online game of his more real than his real life. He doesn't consider the world of living in our basement, eating our food, mooching our Wifi, fighting with people, screeching at the neighbors and going through job after job after job his real life. Home? Is that what he meant on the stairs, that he just wanted to get online?

I say his name. He doesn't answer. I repeat it louder. He doesn't look at me. I am already too late, he is inside of his game. I reach for the knife. He grabs for it. It clatters to the cement floor.

"Leave it!" he says in a voice so low, so growly that I hardly recognize him. I do. There will be nothing gained by picking up the knife. Shelley has often said, "How many times are you going to bail him out of jail before he does some serious damage?" Has that time now come?

Shaking, I kneel beside my brother and place the ends of my fingers lightly on his shoulder. He screeches and arches away as if burned, but for the briefest of moments his attention is diverted away from the voluptuous damsels, the wide shouldered, colorfully armoured knights on white horses, the ornate castles, the open markets selling wine and bread and fish.

"Hey," I say as gently as I can. "What's going on? Talk to me."

When we were boys, brothers in the same house, I would poke at him on purpose. The screams that ensued would have our mother hurrying in from wherever she happened to be. By the time she arrived, I would be sitting calmly in a corner reading my comic book, while he would be thrashing on the floor. Her fury would be directed at my brother and his tantrums, his tantrums for no reason, according to her. It was easy to lose patience with my bedwetting, overweight, smelly brother in those days. It's easy now. My wife Shelley regularly does.

Our mother died when we were both twelve, and eight years later our father succumbed to an overdose of his sleeping meds. He should have died when she did though, because after our mother was gone, he wandered around like something broken. It was me who made pots of Kraft Dinner and boiled hot dogs on the stove while my father shuffled aimlessly through the rooms of the house. It was me who cleaned up after my twin brother's tantrums, repairing walls and windows, doing laundry, washing the sheets of his wet bed. He became my responsibility then. He is my responsibility now.

Shelley and I are having our first baby in four months. Last week she gave me an ultimatum. "Either your brother is out of here by the time the baby comes or I will be."

I'm hoping she doesn't really mean it. I'm hoping it's the hormones talking. I walk around these days with a permanent knot in my stomach. If we kicked him out, where would he go?

How do I tell her that because he's my brother, my twin brother, and that no matter what happens, we are bound to each other? She knew this going in, didn't she? He was supposed to be the best man at our wedding and ended up not showing up for it at all. At the last moment, a friend stepped in. My worry, though, cast a pall over the entire ceremony and reception. On our honeymoon we had our first serious fight, and it was about my brother. All of our fights have been about my brother.

After the wedding I figured I would find him in jail from a fight because someone touched him or made fun of him. That wasn't the case. He'd gotten involved with his online lords and ladies and had simply forgotten. Even the alarms that I set on his computer screen to remind him had gone unheeded. He'd merely turned them off.

"What's going on?" I say quietly into his ear now. "Why are you home so early? You can tell me." I reach out to touch him again but move my hand back before I make contact. He's doing that whimpering thing and I don't need him to go into full tantrum mode. I don't need any more walls kicked in or light fixtures broken.

I back up and sit on the edge of his bed and watch the action on the forty two inch screen. My brother's avatar gallops in from the right of the screen to the center. His avatar figure is a handsome knight on a magnificent, coal black horse. The red insignia on his shield he told me he designed himself. His avatar pauses and has a conversation with a a waif like blonde in a long red cape carrying a basket full of red grapes. From where I am sitting I'm not close enough to read the speech bubbles above their heads. If I were to move closer, my brother would immediately mute the speech and the bubbles would disappear. I'm sure of this.

My brother hasn't always been living with us. After his last court hearing he was put into a halfway house which was a kind of sheltered workshop thing. It didn't last. After he broke the nose of his caretaker, I was called. He moved in with us. Shelley was against it from the start but what could I do? What are we supposed to do? Leave him out in the street? It's just him and me.

Fraternal twins, we look nothing alike. I look over at my brother now, at the bulk of him sitting on the old desk chair that I found for him at the dump, at the way the fat of his hips bulge over the sides of the chair, at the way it creaks under his weight.

His hands move on the keyboard and mouse. More conversation between his avatar and the blonde. An avatar in a jester suit dances around them in a circle. It must be something funny, because I see my brother's shoulders and belly jiggle in mirth. The only time he laughs is when he is in the game.

I glance at my watch. I have to be to work soon, but I can't leave until I know what's going on. But what do I do? Press him for answers? Call his work? The thought of that sends shudders through me.

He pulls out a big bag of potato chips from a drawer in the desk and begins munching. I recognize this bag. Shelley had bought this organic brand when she had some friends over the other night, teachers from her school. She blamed me when she couldn't find the bag.

I move toward him and just as I expected, he mutes the conversation and the speech bubbles disappear. "What happened at work?" I demand.

Without looking away from the screen he says, "They're not nice."

"Maybe not," I say. "But that doesn't mean you can go around bullying people."

"But they're NOT NICE." He glares at me through bulgy eyes which suddenly frighten me, then back at his game.

For a long time I've felt there was something strange about this game. Some of the figures seem less like comic book avatars and more like real people with genuine facial expressions. I've never been able to explain it and when I mention this to Shelley she shakes her head and says that avatars these days do look like real people.

Because I wanted to understand my brother a bit better, a month ago I asked him for the name of the game he's in. When he told me, I went and looked it up online for myself. I didn't want my brother to know, but my plans were to enter the game anonymously just to see what he does in there. I couldn't find it. I even went to a computer store to ask. The young gaming geek down there looked it up for me, and told me that no such game exists.

Weird. Strange. But maybe my brother told me the wrong name. Maybe he just wants something of his own, something that his twin brother isn't going to spy on him about. When he was at work once, I went downstairs, turned his computer on, and on came the game. I didn't want to actually enter the game from his computer, I was sure he'd be able to figure that out somehow. So I wrote the name of it down on the back of my hand, including the URL, but upstairs at my own laptop, I got a 404 error. No such website. No such game.

When I told Shelley she sort of sighed and came up with the simple explanation that I hadn't thought of before. She told me that there are lots of computer games that are private. You need to sign in before you can even get into that section of the internet. "It's sort of like the back streets of the web," she said. I never knew such a place existed.

I know my brother has an imagination. I've known this since we were boys in the same house. Sometimes I wonder if maybe this game is something he's totally made up himself. Does he have the smarts for that? I'm not sure.

When we were little and would ride in the

backseat of our parents' Dodge, we had to drive past a very long metal-roofed chicken barn to get home. Whenever it came into view my brother would say, "I see the lake first!"

"It's not a lake, stupid," I would counter. "It's a building."

My parents in the front seat would say nothing. When I think back on it the seeds of our family's discontent were sown in abundance when we were children. The first born of us twins, I became the good one, the smart one, while he became the crazy one.

"It is a lake." He said this with such vehemence that nobody could argue. Then he would say, "Sometimes things are there that you don't even see."

I would roll my eyes at him and under my breath and mutter, "idiot." It embarrassed me that we were brothers, that we had once shared something so intimate as a womb. I would poke him again. He would scream and scream, and of course get blamed by my parents for "provoking the whole thing."

If you squinted just right the huge metal barn roof did sort of look like a lake in the far distance. I would never admit that.

So, you see, I blame myself for the way my brother turned out. It was my fault really. Probably if I had been kinder to him, if I hadn't hated him so, our parents wouldn't have died. If I hadn't teased him so mercilessly, if I hadn't been there always pushing him down, poking him, touching him, maybe he would have turned out better. Much of it is my fault. All of it is my fault.

Sometimes I wonder if I still hate him. The

doorbell rings. I give my brother a backward glance as I leave his room, but he seems totally disinterested and unconcerned.

Two uniformed policemen want to know if my brother lives here.

"Can I ask what this is about?"

The officers are cookie-cutter moulds of each other with short hair and wide shoulders, one only slightly taller than the other. That's just about the only difference between them. The taller one says, "There was a stabbing."

I swallow. "A stabbing?"

"And a robbery," the other one says.

My mouth goes dry. "What—what happened?"

"Some money's gone missing from the car wash. Your brother was seen running from the place of business with a knife. Is he here?"

I don't answer. Loud sounds are coming from the basement. It startles me. It sounds like my brother is moving furniture down there, but that's impossible.

"May we come in?"

I nod, lick my lips and open the door wide.

"What's that noise?" one of them asks.

I shrug. "I have no idea." I really didn't. My brother doesn't—can't—move furniture on his own. When he needs a desk moved, for example, he pants and groans and sweats and complains until Shelley and I have to go down to help him.

I decide to be honest. "His room is downstairs. Let me go and check on him. See what he's up to. You can wait here."

"No," the shorter one says.

"We have a warrant," the taller one says.

They follow me down the stairs. At the bottom I

think about the blood on the knife and ask, "Was someone hurt?"

"Enough for a trip to the hospital."

A shudder of fear runs through me. "Someone must have touched him. I told the people there—" I didn't finish my sentence.

"Touched him?"

"He doesn't like to be touched."

"Well, he could have killed that man."

I can still hear the heavy sound of furniture moving. When I call his name things suddenly become very still. Too still. Oddly still. I can't hear his heavy breathing, and if he'd been moving furniture, I would hear him breathing. I knock on his closed door. No answer. I knock again, and call for him. Nothing.

"We're coming in!" the tall one says.

That's all we need, for them to go in like a pair of elephants and him crouching behind his desk and holding that huge knife. Gently I turn the knob. It turns but the door won't open. "Hey!" I call his name again. Nothing. I push harder.

"He's shoved some furniture against the door," I tell the officers my voice trembling. If he had enough adrenaline to move all of his furniture against the door, there's no telling what we'll find when we get in there.

"Let's go in," the taller one says.

"One, two, three." The two of them shove their full weight against the door. I help, and with the three of us pushing we manage to open the door a couple of inches. Somehow my brother has moved every bit of his furniture against the door. How had he possibly accomplished this? I peer through the small opening and call his name again. Absolute stillness. But he will be there. There is no way out of his room. This is the only door, and the basement window is set high in the wall and far too small for a man of his heft to wedge through. I call his name again. "Hey. Bro, let us in. No one's going to hurt you. We just need to talk."

I'm afraid. I know how wild he can get when police officers try to slap handcuffs on him. Still no answer. The three of us continue to push, and finally, finally, we are able to squeeze through and climb over pieces of furniture to get into his domain. He has unplugged his computer, and it is on his desk which is shoved up against the door. I manage to get us through without toppling the flat screen monitor.

His room is empty.

"Let me check his bathroom," I say. "That's where he'll be."

I knock on the bathroom door. No answer. Not even a whimper. I open it a crack and say, "Don't be scared. Some people want to ask you a couple of questions. I'm here. Nobody will touch you. Come on out of the shower now."

I pull aside the shower curtain and am stunned when he isn't cowering against the metal walls. I go back out into his room feeling puzzled and strangely afraid. The officers are looking through his bedroom, under the bed, in the closet. I stand in the middle of the room shaking my head and swallowing and telling them that I have no idea where he could have gone, that he is more than three hundred pounds and there isn't any place he could hide, and how did he manage to get out of the room, and then pile furniture against the door from the inside? As well, there is no sign of the knife, the blood. The drips on the cement floor have been wiped clean.

One of the officers has my brother's hard drive tower under one arm. When I look at it he says, "We'll be taking this."

I am too numb to argue. I simply say, "He doesn't have email or Facebook or anything," I say. "All he does is play an online game."

"Still, we'll be taking it. There's the question of that missing money."

When my brother comes back and his computer is gone, he's going to be pissed.

I leave his room and the two follow me while we check through the rest of the rooms in the basement. There is no door to the outside from the basement and all of the windows in basement are tiny rectangles.

He is not in the furnace room. He's not in the room with the washer and dryer. We go into our storage room. He is not hiding behind boxes, or in closets or cubbyholes or in that space under the stairs. I am absolutely dumbfounded and tell them so.

"Obviously he got out while we were in the living room talking," says the short one.

I shake my head. "Then what was all that noise?'

The taller one says, "We've wasted enough time in here. We need to canvas the neighborhood."

When they are satisfied that my brother is not in the house they leave a card on my kitchen table and I promise to call them as soon as my brother comes home.

They leave, taking my brother's computer and his wallet, which was on the desk. I sit down at the table after they leave and text my boss. "Urgent

Family Stuff," I write. "I'll be in as soon as I can."

I think he's used to these messages by now. If things don't improve it'll be me losing my job, not my brother.

As I sit there I begin wondering about something. Had my brother found some sort of secret hiding place in the basement? Is this little tract house part of some big underground labyrinth of passageways? I decide I need to take a better look. People just don't disappear.

I go back downstairs. I call his name. "You can come out now," I say. "They're gone. Come on out and we can talk."

Nothing.

"Hey," I say gently. "They're all gone now. You're safe. Whatever happens, you're safe."

I make my way into the laundry room and examine the wall behind the washing machine. I find no secret doors to secret closets, not anywhere. I continue my search through the other rooms. I will check all of the rooms before I go back into his. His room I will save for last. His room will have every nook and cranny examined and looked through.

When I am in the furnace room, I hear the unmistakeable sounds of his game. I stop and feel a chill. They took his computer hard drive. How can I be hearing his game? As I make my way down the hallway, the sounds are louder. It's the medieval music, the beeps and chimes which signify conversation. I stand in his doorway, stunned.

There on his monitor is his game. The jester is jumping in circles and laughing. When I enter the room, he seems to stop and look at me. Grin at me. Yet, I know this is impossible.

I am rooted to the floor. I cannot move. I simply

stare.

There is the open air market filled with colourful cloth and fruit and meats of all kinds hanging from hooks. I see horses and movement. I hear the sounds of the bazaar. People laughing, talking. Someone is sitting on a rock playing a lute. I do not recognize the tune. Two others are drinking mead from pottery cups. Several children run from stall to stall.

I stare, scarcely able to breathe. Slowly, I make my way to the monitor. Did the police not take the hard drive after all? Had they maybe taken something that resembled the hard drive? Some other piece of equipment? That had to be it.

But this thought moves to horror when I see that the monitor cord is unplugged from the wall. I finger it for several seconds wondering if I am truly going crazy. I plug it in. Nothing changes. I unplug it and it makes no difference to the unfolding scenes. I lay the flat of my hand on the edge of the screen. It feels cold. There is not that warm static you experience when you press your hand against a live screen. Maybe it's my imagination, but the avatars all seem to be gazing at my hand. One of them points at it and laughs. Another seems to look out at me and right into my eyes. I move my hand and back away in horror.

And then I see him trotting in from the left of the screen. I recognize the black horse, the red insignia that he designed himself. I move close to the screen and sit down in my brother's chair and stare at that handsome wide shouldered knight. Riding side-saddle behind him is the blonde with the long red cape. With one hand she holds onto his shoulder and in the other she holds her basket of fruit.

They come to the front of the screen and stop. I cannot move my eyes away. This is my brother. Those are my brother's eyes, his face. Unmistakably, eerily him.

He looks at me for several seconds, grins, and mouths the word, "goodbye." With a wave of his hand they are off. I stare. Something is attached to his belt. I see what it is—the knife.

Mad Scientist

I've suspected for some time that I should go to the authorities about Lewis. Why haven't I? Fear, I suppose. Even anonymous calls aren't anonymous. Both my landline and my cell phone could easily be traced to me. Even a pay phone is out of the question. For example, if I used a pay phone, the call would be tracked back to that particular phone. And witnesses would come forward, witnesses who could identify me making a call at the phone booth at that time. These people have their ways.

Plus, I have the idea that he suspects I know something. So, that's why I need to be circumspect in my dealings with him, and hope (and pray) for a window of opportunity.

Lewis, you see, is a terrorist. Lewis is the worst kind of terrorist, because Lewis is leading a classroom of high school age children down the Taliban path. That's the sad part, the part that makes me know I'm shirking my responsibility by not going to the RCMP immediately with the information I have gathered about Lewis and the goings-on in his classroom.

Lewis is a chemistry teacher in the same fairly

renowned private school where I am employed as a mathematics professor, and my classroom is located directly across the hall from his. So, you see, this gives me an opportunity to note everything that goes on in there.

I have studied these things on the Web. I know the chemicals one must have on hand to build a bomb, and in what proportions. I know the paraphernalia required, the supplies needed. Lewis has all of these in abundance in locked cabinets in his classroom.

You may wonder at my interest. My wife of only three years was killed on 9/11, and if this has sharpened my senses to terrorists activities, then so be it.

Lewis knows my history. I know the way he looks at me when he thinks I'm unaware he's there. I see the way he regards me across the hall with that pouty mouth of his, one eyebrow raised, hand on one hip. The way he stares at me in the staff room and addresses me with, "So, Maurice, you're young. When are you going to think about getting married again?"

That he would bring up the subject infuriates me!

I've chosen not to remarry. Terrorists like him would like me to. They would like to me to get on with my life, but I won't give him or the terrorists the satisfaction. When I told him that, when I told him I hated all people, everywhere of Arab descent, he seemed taken aback.

"I'm shocked," he said, eyes wide. "Many of them are good people. How can you say that?"

How can I say that? After what happened to my wife, how can he even wonder? It was then that I began to observe him. I live my life carefully looking for that window. But while I wait, I am forced to endure the smells from his room, the inane chatter, the music that he insists on playing. There are times I can almost taste the various reeks of the bomb making chemicals in there. More than once I have gone home sick to my stomach at the stench of it all. Plus my dreams are filled with his high pitched voice calling to his students, "Measure carefully kids, or you'll blow us all to kingdom come. Heh, heh." That chuckle and those words should tell you everything.

In my dreams I watch him sashay between his classroom tables on toes, as if in dancing slippers, his grey streaked ponytail whipping from side to side. In one recurring dream, he leans over and smirks at me, his lab coat falling forward to reveal a chest full of bombs.

Dreams or no dreams, I tell you, sometimes I am downright terrified of the man. I truly am. If you could see the gleam in his eye, I know you would agree with me. Plus, I have done a little digging. I have learned a fact about Lewis that few people know. One evening after everyone had gone home, I was able to get into the school's confidential files.

I discovered something profoundly unsettling. Early on in his career, two students suffered minor injuries when a chemistry experiment in his lab went horribly wrong. According to the report, it was not Lewis's fault. Two years later, the same thing happened. Again, he was deemed not culpable. Students had stayed after school, unsupervised while they worked on a science fair project. At the end of it all, he felt responsible (as well he should), took a year's leave of absence and spent some time in a psychiatric hospital. Psychiatric hospital, my foot. I know how these terrorist cells work. I know what he was really doing during that time.

Since I discovered Lewis's past history, something strange has happened. Somehow he has figured out what I know, and his rampages have become increasingly personal, directed at me.

This morning I came to school to find my entire desk in disarray. I always keep finally sharpened pencils in the rectangular compartment in the middle drawer of my desk. These are laid side by side next to the mechanical pencils and the ballpoint pens, always with their sharpened ends toward the left. I have arranged them thusly, so when I pick them up with my right hand, they are ready for immediate use. Next to them are my mathematical instruments, the compass, the protractors and the other accoutrements of my profession. Beyond them, in the larger compartment, I keep boxes of staples, note pads, sheets of graph paper and an assortment of rulers, including a slide rule and a number of scientific calculators. To find the pens in disarray, to find them interspersed amongst each other, to find three of the number two lead pencils blunted, I was frankly, horrified. The effect was one of violation, not unlike I imagined that of being raped. I immediately went to the headmaster, who asked if anything had been taken.

Taken! No, nothing was taken. Nothing except my security, my safety. My sanctuary. When I suggested that it might be Lewis, he said, "Why would Lewis do that?"

"Because he's a—" I almost blurted out the word terrorist! But I held my tongue.

I made my way back to my classroom, and there

was that scoundrel standing in the hallway arranging student science fair displays. This is supposed to be a high school, yet these displays look as if done up by preschoolers. This is science? This is what parents pay for? I remind myself that this isn't where he shines. His expertise lies in bomb making, and what a perfect cover, a chemistry teacher.

"Morning, Maurice," he called to me. He was up on tiptoes, taping a picture to the high wall. I merely nodded. He will ruin the walls with that tape of his, I was thinking. I was going to make a comment, there and then, but thought better of it. Time enough to bring it up at the staff meeting.

He came down to flat feet. "Just thought I'd brighten up thc old halls of learning."

I turned away from him.

Plus, his classroom! I need to describe that room. Through his door—which he insists on keeping open at all times—I note the disorganization, students walking willy-nilly, jars perched precariously on mucky tables. How can anyone live like that? No wonder two students almost died. My own classroom, by contrast, is orderly, and my students know exactly what is expected of them. I glanced at the locked metal door to the bomb cupboard.

A week later, another incident. I had returned from my usual quiet lunch in the corner of the staff room to find that my class instructions, which I had meticulously written on the corner of the blackboard – Homework, Chapter 18, Sections 1 and 2, Including the Bonus questions – had been completely obliterated from the board. Lewis had done this to warn me. What he was saying was back off, keep what you know to yourself.

But I shall not! I shall not! I will wait for the window.

And this time I had proof. Moments before, I had seen Lewis emerging from my classroom. I walked over to his room, forced myself to enter that den of disorder and said, "Lewis. A word."

He strode toward me, all concern. "Yes, Maurice?"

"You were in my classroom, I believe."

"Yes, I guess I was." He was rubbing his hands together. Well, of course he would, to get rid of the chalk dust!

"May I ask what you were doing in there?"

He raised his eyebrows. I stood waiting. He laughed. I hate that laugh of his, nervous and high-pitched, like a whinnying horse. Then he flipped his ponytail behind him and put his hands into his pockets under his dirty lab coat. I started. For a moment, I expected him to pull out a gun or reveal a chest strapped with dynamite.

But he pulled out his hands, scratched his nose and looking at me expectantly, like a child he said, "You're serious."

"Yes. I am. Most definitely." I stood my ground. It's important to stand one's ground when dealing with people like Lewis.

"I was talking to Anna Greene. She's your student, she also happens to be mine. We were discussing the set for the play."

I turned on my heels and walked out. The set for the play! And if you believe that, I have a bridge for sale. Back in my classroom, it took me several minutes of rearranging my things before I could calm myself enough to begin the mathematics lecture.

Lewis's torments increased after that. I began seeing him everywhere, hovering near my classroom, following me into the staff room. Once I even spied him bending over my car in the staff parking lot. I accosted him about that one, and here's what he said, "Your Austin. A beautiful car, Maurice. You've kept it in nice shape."

"Yes," I said, unlocking the driver side door and climbing in.

At home, I discovered that Lewis had even been there. He had actually come right to the front door of my home. There was a small pile of dog manure on my porch. Who but Lewis and his sick mind would've put it there?

"Is this what they teach you in Taliban school?" I yelled to the heavens. But I could not be sure this was just manure so I donned a double layer of rubber gloves to check through it. It would be just like the terrorists to hide in the muck, a bit of plastic explosive. It seemed harmless, but what it gave me was a new revelation. Lewis expected me to think that there was something in this and make me paw through it. He was probably at home right now, laughing at the whole ordeal.

Lewis, the ultimate actor, feigned complete innocence when I approached him the following morning. Chemistry? He should be teaching drama!

"Do you like shit?" I asked him quietly in the staff room.

"Do I like shit?" He turned slowly to face me and said the whole thing again, elongating the last two words, saying it loud enough for everyone to hear. "Do I like shit?"

"Yes. You think it's funny to put things in it, or not put things in it?" I kept my voice down while I stirred the sugar lump into my coffee. I watched his reaction carefully.

Lewis shook his head at me, sighed and walked away. But I could see it! I could! A tiny tic of nervousness, an anxious squinting at the corner of one eye. I'm on to him!

The last straw, the final straw occurred a week later, when I left the house one morning to find that one of the tires on my Austin was flat.

"Lewis, you have gone too far this time!"

I trudged back inside through the gathering storm and called a cab. I should've known when I saw Lewis admiring my car. I should've known he was planning something like this.

When the cab arrived, driven by a scruffy little man who smelled bad, I seethed all the way to town. It's a good fifteen minute drive at the best of times, and the cabby seemed in no particular hurry, despite my protests that I'd better things to do then to sit in the back seat of his foul smelling vehicle.

By the time I arrived, school had already begun. It was raining heavily.

"Lewis, you will pay for this!" I muttered as I slopped through puddles, cursing myself for forgetting my rubbers. I hurried down the hall, my shoes squawking with the wet. Outside of my still locked mathematics door, my students were lounging against the walls. Some of them were snickering.

"Mr. Schechtor, don't you know it's bad luck to have an open umbrella in a building," one of the girl students said.

"Thank you," I said, "for those words of consummate wisdom."

One of the tall girls tittered. I stared hard at her

and unlocked the door. I was in no mood. Across the hall Lewis stood in his doorway and called cheerily, "Morning, Maury."

Maury? He is calling me Maury now?

A month after the car incident, fate handed me that window.

The two of us were at school late in the evening, when Lewis came into my classroom and right up to my desk. He was all smiles when he said, "I see the two of us are burning the midnight oil. How about when we finish here, we go out and grab a beer?"

Grab a beer, indeed! I barely looked up when he said this but continued grading my papers. He was halfway out the door when I remembered the pipe and Bic lighter I always keep at the ready in my breast pocket and yelled, "Wait!"

He turned, clearly startled at my outburst.

"How about on the roof?" I said.

"Excuse me?"

"How about we go up on the roof? I was actually going to head up there in a bit to have a smoke." I patted my pipe and smiled. I actually smiled at him. "I'll make a pot of tea in the staff room and take it up to the roof and meet you there," I said.

"Well, sure," he said stroking his ponytail. How I hate that man for what he did to my Mary.

There is a deck of sorts on the roof of this old school. It's strictly off-limits to students, but staff use it, and there are several chairs and a picnic table up there.

I made a pot of tea, carried it up the steps to the roof and sat in the cool breeze at the top of the building waiting for him. I put the pipe in the middle of the table.

Then finally he was there, scraping his chair back and sitting down, flipping his ponytail behind him and chatting about how nice this was, just the two of us. And how he'd been looking forward to talking to me and he'd been wanting for a long time to clear up what ever it was between the two of us.

"Stop," I put my hand. I could stand no more of this. "Stop right now."

He blinked at me and promptly closed his mouth. The pipe lay there between us. "Smoke it," I told him.

"What?" He looked at me aghast.

"I said smoke it."

"I don't smoke."

I leaned toward him and pointed to the pipe. "Pick it up. Smoke it."

His scrawny Adam's apple bobbled up and down as he swallowed rapidly. "What's going on, Maury? What's this about?" A tiny tongue of spittle snaked down his chin. The winds lifted his ponytail. I could tell he was nervous. Good.

"You know exactly what this is about," I said. "Consider this revenge. For the death of my Mary."

"Mary? Your wife, Mary? What do I have to do with Mary?"

"Take the pipe."

"No, thank you. I don't know what this is about, but no thank you." He got up, and I grabbed the pipe and my lighter and went to the railing, where he was leaning against it looking out over the city. It was on to Plan B, but that was okay.

"I don't understand it," he said turning to face me. "Why you seem to hate me. I've tried to be nice to you, I've gone out of my way—"

"Why do I hate you? Now there's a question." I

leaned far over the railing. Up the road, a garbage truck was rumbling its way down toward us. I smiled. Fate was indeed on my side tonight. I leaned over farther, tried to calculate when the truck would thunder past to mask the sound—

"Maury, I wouldn't exactly trust that railing." He was quite close to me now and was touching my jacket. To pull me to safety? With one quick motion, I pulled the pipe from my pocket, lit it, and shoved it deep within his shirt pocket, so quickly, so suddenly that he didn't have time to react. In one motion, I heaved him over the railing. He screamed, looking back at me in shock as he fell.

"Fly! Fly!" I called after him. As the truck roared past, covering the sound, the pipe bomb exploded. He had blown into a million pieces before he hit the ground. I watched the truck. It didn't stop. They hadn't seen anything, or if they had, they would merely have thought it was a light flickering in a window—

***

I was back in my own house, drinking tea before anyone realized he was gone.

The following morning when I entered the staff room for my morning coffee, a group of somber faces looked up at me from around the table. The fresh out of college girls' gym teacher was there, her head was down, her shoulders heaving.

"What's the matter?" I asked cheerfully. "Somebody die?" My voice was jocular, full of gaiety.

She looked up at me with red rimmed eyes. "Haven't you heard? Lewis is dead."

I raised my eyebrows, attempting to look concerned.

The biology teacher said, "As near as anyone can tell, it was suicide. His body was found this morning beside the school. He made a homemade bomb with the chemicals from his lab and then jumped off the building last night. Who would ever have thought he would do that?"

"He was working late here," another said.

I held my coffee cup steadily in my hand. Not a drop would spill.

The little lady gym teacher said, "He was going through a rough time recently. His wife left him and took their daughter. It was hard on him. But I can't believe it came to this."

"The students all loved him. This will devastate them." This came from the Home Economics teacher.

The police came. They questioned me intensely. Yes, I was here last night. Yes, working in my classroom the entire evening. No, I never noticed anything out of the ordinary. I keep my door closed, you see. Yes, I knew Lewis quite well, and yes, he had been going through a rough time of late. His wife had left him. Taken their daughter. Yes, I would say he did seem suicidal to me. Yes, most definitely. We were all concerned for him, all of us. And yes, several times I'd seen him working late on something in his lab. When I would go in and ask him about it, he tried to hide it, not that I would know anything about bombs. No problem at all, officer, glad to be of assistance.

I realized that I couldn't tell the authorities that I'd just killed a noted terrorist. Most of these local authorities are in bed with the Taliban. But I knew what had happened. There was one less terrorist on the planet.

Already news cameras were filming the students hugging each other on the grounds, tears coursing down their precious cheeks. Oh, this will make for maudlin television, I thought. Hello, Oprah.

And suddenly I was thinking about fingerprints that I must've left on the door to the roof. Casually, ever so casually, I made my way up the stairs to the roof. A uniformed policeman was there, a young nervous looking man with darting eyes. Before he could stop me I ducked under the yellow crime scene tape and grasped, firmly, the doorknob to the roof. I made sure he saw me do that.

"Sir," he said, "Sir, no one is allowed up there. This is a crime scene."

"Oh, dear, of course. I didn't realize. I'm so sorry. I'm not myself this morning. Lewis was a dear friend, you see. You'll have to forgive me. I wanted to put flowers at the site." And I held out the straggly bouquet of weeds I had just scrounged from the cracks in the pavement out front.

***

A year has passed. There is a new chemistry teacher at school, a large woman who wears denim jumpers and Birkenstocks. I ignore her and she ignores me. But Lewis has found a way to torment me from the grave. At night I hear a sound like a roaring in my head, a choir of Lewis voices, as if Lewis has become many Lewises, hundreds of Lewises all calling out to me in unison, "Fly. Fly, fly Maury. Come back up to the rooftop and fly! Burst into a thousand pieces like me and fly."

I have taken to sleeping with the radio on at night, tuned between stations, but Lewis has found a way to speak through the white noise. "I can fly.

Watch me. Watch me—"

"Quiet!" I cover my head with my pillow. "Leave me alone!"

But the voices have only multiplied. I hear them when I am in the middle of a mathematics lecture. I hear them when I am pushing a cart in the grocery store, the wheels squeaking on the tiled floor. "The rooftop, Maury— The rooftop, Maury— The rooftop, Maury." I can hear them when I am stopped at a red light or driving through traffic, or sitting in a staff meeting. "Come to the roof— Come to the roof— Come to the roof. Watch me fly— Watch me fly—"

His harassments also, have not stopped with his death. Little things. Always little things, he does. My toilet paper roll placed wrong way on the holder. My toothpaste tube squeezed from the middle. Lettuce I have just purchased, spotted and weathered in my fridge. Fresh cheese replaced with old blueing blocks. Milk in my fridge, not even my brand, soured and with lumps. Homework erased from the board. Students coming in with the wrong assignments. "Section Twenty-Three," I yell at them. "I assigned Section Twenty-Three, but all of you have done Section Twenty-Four! How is it that you have all done Section Twenty-Four?"

"You assigned us Section Twenty-Four," they tell me, looking at each other in wonder. "You wrote it on the board yesterday."

I didn't, of course, but there is no use in arguing. It is Lewis who is doing this to me.

Tonight as I sit here at my desk, my classroom is in shambles. I am writing, writing, but the lead in my pencil keeps breaking. Papers are strewn across the floor. Books are upside down. Students desks are upended. The chalkboard is full of nonsensical scribbles. I cannot clean up fast enough from Lewis's tirades. They are getting worse.

He is above me now, dancing on the roof, prancing in those little black shoes of his. I yell loudly for him to stop, stop, but he does not. The dancing continues. I must go up there. To tell him to stop. To make him stop. I must do this. Must go— Must go up to the roof and make him stop. Fly with me, Maury, fly with me. I pat my breast pocket, where I have made another bomb, and ascend the stairs.

Strange Faces

The Hockey Bag

Just trying to be Mr. Nice Guy. Just trying to keep my nose clean and where does it get me? Trouble with a capital T. But let me go back. Let me start at the very beginning.

It's Tuesday and it's dark and I'm on my Harley heading home from work. Up ahead I pick up this weird looking reflection in my headlights. When I get closer I can see it's a ribbon of reflective tape on some sort of a huge bag down in the ditch beside the road. I pull over and I'm thinking to myself, "Okay Skinner, what is that?" That's my name by the way, Skinner, James Skinner, but mostly everybody calls me Skinner or Jim. Back in school I got "Skinny" a lot, and maybe that's what gave me such an attitude. But all that's behind me now. I'm making a new life for myself. But I'll talk about that later.

I hop off my bike and am going down for the bag, when all of a sudden there's this cold wind just coming out of nowhere. Like its been waiting for me or something. Like I've been beamed into some weird rerun of *The Shining*. Like I'm on the set of *The Cabin in the Woods*. There is this little voice inside me saying, "Skinner, get your sorry arse back up on your bike and get home."

I should've listened.

Instead, I drag up the humongous, heavy bag and shine my headlight on it. It's big and blue with *Sportchek* in six inch letters across the top. It's got one of those industrial size zippers on it which run around the middle. I take hold of one side of the zipper and yank it open. Hockey equipment. That's all. What did I expect, a body?

I dig through the stuff. The guy whose bag it is, is a goalie. The leg pads aren't there, but everything else is–trapper, blocker, helmet, pants and a few articles of clothing. I play in a beer league so I ought to know. The guy's gonna be some pissed when he realized he lost it. Fell off the back of his truck most likely.

I bungee cord the thing to the back of my Harley. It's heavy and awkward and I'll probably get stopped by the cops on the way home, so what else is new?

Marcie isn't home when I get there. She's taken Olivia over to her sister Cheryl's.

Did I tell you about that? I'm married now and I got a one-year-old kid. I told you I'd turned over a new leaf. I even got me a steady job up in the warehouse. Job's pretty boring, but it pays the bills and the guys I work with are okay. If you could've seen me when I was eighteen, nineteen you'd never know I was the same guy.

At home I lug the bag off my bike into our duplex, and then I make a sandwich and grab a beer. While I'm munching on my ham and cheese, I think of the poor guy who lost all his hockey gear and I decide to check if there's some ID. I lift the smelly pieces out one at a time and lay them on the floor.

There's no ID anywhere. Nowhere. So I pack everything back up and stash it in the back corner of our storage room. I know what I should do, what you're supposed to do when you find lost stuff that's worth something—you're supposed to take it to the police. But the police and me? We don't have a great history.

Three days later I still haven't called the cops. Marcie is kind of getting on my case about it, too. "It smells like a cat peed on it," she says.

On the fourth day, Saturday, I'm sitting across from Marcie at our kitchen table drinking coffee. She's wearing tight jeans and one of those little tank tops of hers that I like. Her brown hair is hanging all down around her shoulders the way I like it instead of up in a ponytail. She's staring at me with this serious look in her eyes, and ignoring Olivia who's sitting in her high chair banging with a spoon, and getting cereal muck everywhere.

"Jim," she says, "If you're afraid to call the cops, why not just take the bag over to the arena and leave it there?"

"I ain't afraid to call the cops." I get up to pour more coffee.

"Well, it seems to me like you are."

"I'm not afraid to call the cops, I just don't like cops. They'll think I stole it or something. They'll make it my fault. They always do."

"That's just stupid." She lifts Olivia out of her high chair and cleans off her face with a wet washcloth and says to her, "You need a bath, pumpkin face."

With Marcie and Olivia in the bathroom, I open up our laptop and get into Craig's List. Maybe whoever it was who lost his bag put an ad in here somewhere. I look and look and then I see it, the second item in the "lost" column—

"Large Sportchek blue hockey bag." And then a number.

"Hey Marcie," I say jotting down the number on the back of an envelope.

She can't hear me, what with Katy Perry blaring from the bathroom radio and Marcie singing along and Olivia googling. In our bedroom I shut the door, sit on the end of the bed and call the number. One ring later, I get a voice mail: "This is 555–4434. Leave your name and number." Stern voice. Not a friendly voice.

"Hi. My name's Skinner. Jim Skinner. I think I found your hockey bag." I give him my cell number and hang up.

Next day at work, I'm hanging up my jacket in the coffee room when I look down at the newspaper on the table. Normally, I'm not hooked into the news so much, but the front page is filled top to bottom with a story about some woman who got herself murdered. There's an ambulance and police cars and you can just make out the corner of a stretcher where her body is covered with just a bit of blue peeking out. I skim the story. And then I stop. Dead.

Her body was found right where I found the hockey bag. I'm not joking. I read it more carefully. The same night I found the hockey bag was the night they figured she was murdered.

Coincidence? One's got nothing to do with the other? Maybe. Or maybe not. I fold up the paper and shove it into my back pack. I would study the whole thing later.

I can't sleep that night, thinking about that hockey equipment still in our storage closet.

Next morning Marcie says she and Cheryl are planning to take the babies and head over to the mall. Okay with me. I'm too keyed up to walk around the mall. I'll spend the day working on my bike. Somehow, I never get around to telling Marcie about the dead person or the ad or the phone call. When she and Olivia emerge from the baby's room, Marcie's got her hair tied back up into a ponytail. She hands Olivia to me while she goes on and on about stuff she wants to buy, and do I want her to pick up anything for me? Yeah, I do. I write it all down for her while Olivia grabs at my ears and nose, and giggles.

All morning I work on my bike, I change the oil, wash it down, shine it up. I'm trying to get my mind on other things. I use my last litre of oil and I'm glad Marcie is picking up more. Around 1:30 my stomach's telling me it's time for lunch so I head inside to see what's in the fridge.

I decide to have another look at that hockey equipment. The guy should be phoning up any minute now, shouldn't he? I try to shake off the feeling I get every time I think about that equipment, and that girl that got killed pretty close to where I found the bag. The two have nothing to do with each other. Yeah. Keep telling yourself that.

I drag out the bag and pull out the trapper and blocker and helmet. It makes me feel weird that a dead body was down in the ravine the whole time I'm dragging this stupid bag up to the road.

I lift up the pants, black with a dirty white stripe down the leg. Nice stuff. There's something hard near the waist band of the pants. Strange. It almost feels like it, whatever it is, is stuffed between the cloth and the padding. I find a place where the steam has been ripped near the waistband and I spread it apart with my fingers. There *is* something down there. I reach in. Carefully, slowly, I pull it out. It's hard all right. Hard and metal. I look at it then, sitting innocently in my hand and I think I'm either going to throw up or faint.

Wrapped up in a piece of flimsy blue material is a gun. I walk around the room breathing deep, still holding this thing in my hand, the blue swishing around my legs until it falls to the floor. Shaking, I drop the thing on the carpet and I scramble for it. What if it's loaded? I pick it up and look at it more closely. It's a Colt Detective Special, a 38. What they might call a Saturday Night Special. Now's not the time to ask me how I know this. I examine it carefully. Only one fired shell. Five good ones left. A loaded gun in my house. With my wife and little kid!

Clumsily I wrap the piece of cloth around the gun again and lay it on the coffee table. My sandwich is still there, but I'm not hungry anymore. Then something niggles at the corner of my thinking. I grab the paper from where I stashed it underneath my side of the bed and look down at the front page again. She, whoever she is, who got herself killed, was wearing blue. I'm holding a gun wrapped in blue. I may not be a rocket scientist, but I can put two and two together as good as the next guy.

I'm going to be sick. I stumble into the bathroom and lean over the toilet. Up it comes, everything I ate for breakfast. A little while later I get up, still breathing hard. I flush the toilet and press both hands against the mirror over the sink. I don't even recognize the mug that looks out at me, my red face coated with sweat. In the corner of the mirror I see someone gliding towards me from the kitchen. It's hockey masked Jason carrying a chainsaw, a blood spattered blue scarf tied around his neck. I groan, run the tap and splash my face with cold water until the image disappears from the mirror. Without towelling off my face, I stumble back into the living room.

I get onto our laptop and the news and read the story of the murder from start to finish. The body was discovered on Friday. She was last seen leaving for work Tuesday at five. That's great I think just great. Where was I Tuesday night? Worked late, picked up a burger at Mickey D's and came home. Marcie and Olivia were at Cheryl's until almost midnight and I'm home alone with no alibi. And me with my prints all over the blasted gun. I can hear the whole thing now:

Cop #1: Okay, Skinner where were you Tuesday night?

Me: Home

Cop #2: Alone?

Me: Yeah, like the movie.

Cop #1: Don't get smart.

Me: I didn't do anything.

Cop #1, motioning to cop #2: Get the cuffs, Ray, we got a live one.

Let's face it, I am knee-deep in cow patties. I have the murder weapon in my house with my prints all over it and to top it all off there's the real murderer out there knowing not only my name, but my number.

My cell phone vibrates in my pocket. I jump a mile! That's him, the murderer–Jason, Hannibal Lecter, Carrie, Chucky, the guy from *The Shining*, a whole cemetery full of vampires. But no. I look down at my phone and sigh with relief. Marcie.

"Hey babe."

"Jim, what's wrong?"

"What do you mean?"

"You sound all funny."

"I'm fine." But I'm not. I'm shaking like a baby. My breath is coming out of me like there's not enough air in the room. I can barely hold the phone in my sweaty hands. "Just got something caught in my throat," I add.

"Jim? I'm at Walmart. What kind of oil did you want again?"

"Um. Yeah. Oil." Breathe in. Breathe out. Think. Think.

"Guy here says you probably want either GTX 20–50 or the GTX 10–30. But, I can't read your writing. I thought I better call you just to make sure, you know?"

"Um—" Think. Think. "Get me the 20-50. Four litres."

"You sure you're okay?"

"Yeah. Fine."

"You sure? You sound funny. You want me to come home?"

No! "No." I need a plan. I need a plan. "I'm fine. I was outside. I think I just got a little weird in the sun."

"Jim?"

"Yeah?"

"It's not sunny out."

After we say goodbye, I begin pacing. First of all I got to get rid of the gun. That's number one. I wrap it up tightly in the blue fabric and try to stuff it back down into the waist band of the hockey pants. It seems like it was easier coming out that it was going in, and that gets me all up in a shaky sweat all over again.

A few minutes later I'm wearing rubber gloves and sitting at the kitchen table wiping the gun with a damp dish towel and re-wrapping it in the blue scarf. Here's my plan—I put the gun back the way I found it. When the guy calls back I'll hand the full bag over to him, all innocent like.

"Your hockey bag? No problem. I picked it up, never even looked inside it. Nope. Not one little peek."

Yeah right. And then he'll come back at midnight and kill us all in our beds. No good. No good. I'm pacing. I walk around all afternoon. He knows where I live! *I friggin' called him! He's got my number!*

Around five Marcie gets home, hands me the stuff she bought and says, "You sure you're okay? You look kind of, I don't know, tired, maybe?"

"I'm fine." I cough a little for effect and forcibly keep myself from looking at our storage closet.

Marcie's holding Olivia and the kid reaches out for me, giggling. I take her and throw her up in the air a few times and she laughs. I tell Marcie that I think maybe we should go out to McDonald's for supper and then come back and watch a movie together.

Much later, with Olivia in bed, we snuggle on the couch with a bowl of buttered popcorn watching the latest super-hero movie. This is better. This is much better. I can almost forget that the guy never called. Never left a message. I feel that horror movie chill coming on me again and snuggle closer to Marcie. She says, "You're freezing!"

"Yeah, freezing. Warm me up."

The guy doesn't call the next day. Marcie and

Olivia go to church in the morning and I sit at the kitchen table drinking, I don't know how many cups of coffee and reading straight through all the online accounts I can find about the murder. I learn the name of the murdered girl, Melissa Anders. She was twenty-two, a university student and she worked at a place called Margaret's Pub downtown. I stare at her picture. She's a pretty girl.

"I got to tell you something," I say to Marcie when she gets home. "It's real important."

"Hey! Hey!" She says grabbing my cigarette right out of my hand and chucking it into the sink. "Since when did you start smoking again, huh?"

"Marcie, listen, I—"

"What are you doing smoking in here?" She's staring at me hard. "With Olivia in here? We don't even let our friends smoke in our house. Not with the baby! What do you think you're doing?"

"Sorry, Marcie, but—"

"The only buts are you butting out, mister." She's backing away from me and her eyes are wide.

I take the car to work the next morning leaving Marcie without a vehicle, but as I tell her, I can't legally ride my bike with that bag bungied to the back. And, I say, "I'm going to take that bag to the police tomorrow."

"Well, it's about time."

Actually, I'm afraid of hockey-masked Jason seeing me around town with his bag strapped to the back of my bike. I lock the bag in the trunk while I'm at work, and all day I'm thinking—what if someone picks today to steal my car? In the end I can't think of a plan, so I just leave the bag in the trunk.

Marcie has spaghetti going when I get home. I kiss her and tell her that the police have the bag now the problem is over. Just before supper I go into the bathroom, lock the door and punch the murderer's number into my cell. No answer. I try again. Each time the voicemail kicks in, I hang up.

"Marcie," I say casually walking back into the kitchen.

"Yeah?"

"I need to take the car to work the next couple of days, until I can finish with the bike."

"Fine with me."

"And, Marcie—"

"Yeah?"

"There are some real weirdos out there. The cops told me that. They told me that if anybody calls here saying that I have his bag, just say, "The police are taking care of this now.""

"The police are taking care of this now," she says in a deadpan. Marcie's no slouch. She's going to know something's up unless I'm smooth.

During supper, there's a Crimestoppers reenactment on the TV. We're sitting at the kitchen table, me and Marcie, and I don't even want to describe what Olivia looks like when she's eating spaghetti. And I'm rising and shushing everybody with a wave of my hand.

A blonde girl in a blue dress is standing at a bus stop. "Tuesday evening Melissa Anders left work and was seen by several people as she waited to catch the bus on Main Street. Her body was found the following morning in the river near Mountain Road." And then the camera pans the river near where I found that bag. "If you have any information leading to an arrest, please call the Crimestoppers hotline."

Yeah. Right. As if.

Marcie wants to walk to the Convenience store for disposable diapers. Do I want to go? I shake my head. Too much to do, I say. Too much to do.

"Suit yourself." She plunks a smiley Olivia into the stroller and off they go.

While they're out, I get the bag out of the trunk and stuff it under the back steps. It's big, but I move some junk up against it and manage to hide it behind a few cinder blocks and boards. Not very original. Police love looking under people's porches. It's the first place they go.

Two more days and still no call. I call Jason—I've started thinking of him as Jason—every chance I get. No one ever answers. Also, there's no more voice mail. Once I let the thing ring ten times. I'm getting edgy.

Every day I come home and worry about the bag. What if Marcie goes under the porch and finds it? Not that she would, but what if she does? I'm trying always to be Mr. Casual. The whole thing's beginning to get to me. People at work come at me and I jump, and at home Marcie's on my case.

"What's with you lately?" she asks me one day.

"Nothing!"

"Don't tell me nothing, Jim Skinner. You've been acting weird for a week so don't you tell me nothing. I come home and you're smoking—" She turns and faces me, wooden soup spoon in her hand raised like a weapon, eyes wide. "No Jim! Tell me no!"

"No, what?"

"You're not using again are you? You're not back to that again are you?"

Before she finishes I put my hands up. "No! No, I promise. It's nothing like that."

"Because if you are—If you are, Jim Skinner—"

I don't let her finish. I'm out the door and on my bike and heading out, feeling miserable, like I've let everyone down. I've got a beautiful wife I don't deserve and a daughter who should have a smart father, not a smart-ass father.

Next thing I know I'm sitting down with a draft and a plate of buffalo wings at Margaret's Pub on Main St.

"Can I get you anything else?" It's a kid who waits on me and he looks not much more than eighteen with pink cheeks and short carrot curls all over his head. His voice is high pitched and squeaky, like it hasn't changed yet. Maybe it hasn't.

"I'm fine."

I'm thinking about voices then. I'm pretty sure I would remember the voice on the phone, clipped, each syllable sounded out, like the guy was constipated. I plunk some money down on the table and wander slowly back towards the can listening to all the waiters I can. None of them sound like Jason, not exactly.

It was a long shot anyway.

When I get back, Marcie is sitting very quietly. The TV is on. She doesn't look at me when I sit down next to her, in fact, if anything she leans away from me.

"You shouldn't have left like that," she says, still not looking at me. I can see she's been crying.

"I know. I'm sorry." Oh man! How do I explain any of this to her? How do I explain that the cops would never, not in two million years, believe my story? How do I tell her that she's the best thing that ever came into my life and I can't lose her?

"Don't do it again," she says. "Don't ever walk out on us again."

"I won't. I promise. I just— There's something I—."

She turns takes my face in her hands. "Jim, I know you're not on drugs. I know it. I know deep down you're a good man."

Now, I know I don't deserve her. I sigh and look down.

A little while later, I ask her, "If you have a phone number of a guy, but you don't have his name or address, is there a place you can get this off the internet? I've looked and I can't figure out where."

"Which guy?"

"What do you mean, which guy?"

"Who's the guy you want the address for?"

"I'm just saying if you had a number could you get an address from it?"

"Oh, so you mean it's hypothetical?"

"Yeah." Whatever that means.

"It depends on if the number's blocked or not."

I bring out the little slip of the paper with Jason's phone number on it and hand it to her. "This is the number I can't find."

"Who is it?"

"Some guy at work." I don't look at her when I say this.

She gets up and grabs our laptop, which she uses way more than me and opens up a program and plugs in a number. She says, "I got an address for it. No name."

"An address is good."

Two days later I'm driving, hockey bag stashed once again in the trunk, out to an address off Fourth Street. As near as I can figure by the numbers on the mail box, the place I'm looking at is that dark green rundown box of a house with a sagging front porch.

I knock on the door. There doesn't seem to be a doorbell. Even if there was, I would have my doubts whether the thing would work. There's no grass anywhere, just a dirt encrusted brown lawn in which any bit of green has long been scraped off by dogs or kids. I find it hard to believe that constipated "Jason" would live in a dump like this.

I knock again. Harder this time. My knock seems to echo inside the place. Maybe it's deserted. I peer through the grimy windows and get this vision of "Jason" sitting there on the couch, hockey mask on, chain saw oiled and ready, and waiting for me.

Gingerly, I try the door. Unlocked. I peer inside. "Hey? Anyone home? Hello!"

No answer. I step inside. All I can hear is my breathing. The interior is dark and smells like used gym socks and old cat litter boxes. When my eyes adjust, I look around. Pizza boxes and McDonald's and Wendy's wrappers lay haphazardly on the floor, the coffee table and arms of the chairs. A skinny cat starts meowing around my legs. It startles me.

Did I have any idea what I was doing here? Did I have a plan? Sort of. Not really.

"WHAT DO YOU THINK YOU'RE DOING HERE?"

I jump and spin around quickly. The voice belongs to a female, a tall female person. A very big female. A female with spiky blonde hair and muscles. No kidding. Muscles. I didn't know women were even capable of six-pack abs. She's wearing one of those body suits like wrestlers wear. Me Tarzan. You Jane.

"Uh. Looking for the guy who lives here?"

"Well, he ain't here." She has that kind of raspy voice that woman have who smoke too much. She puts her hands on her hips and looks at me. Looks down at me, more like.

"You know where he is?" I ask timidly up at her.

"What do you want him for?"

"I have something that's his."

"What?"

"Uh," I pause. "His hockey bag."

"What!" Her eyes flash. She lunges toward me. "What do you mean you have his hockey bag?"

I level my eyes at her. That's what they teach you in Bad Guy School. Don't flinch. Maintain eye contact.

"Were you the guy who called? What are you, threatening me? What do you want? Money? Is this about blackmail? Well, look around yourself buddy, if you came here for money I ain't got a lot to give."

She's laughing now, but underneath it I see something else there—fear. The big woman in front of me is afraid. Even though I'm confused— Blackmail? What is she talking about?—I decide to play it cool. You also learn that in Bad Guy School.

"No," I say. "I just want to give him back his hockey stuff."

She's eyeing me. She's shaking more than me. "Why are you doing this to me? Who *are* you? Why did you call like that right out of the blue?"

Time for a little pause while I try to collect my thoughts. *Out of the blue?* I say, "How 'bout I just wait for him here?" I sit down on a not too clean couch and the cat jumps on my lap and purrs. The big woman is pacing and making fists. "The bum," she says. "You can wait all you want, he ain't coming back. Never. And I don't know who you are."

I'm starting to get a weird little glimmer of an idea. "You were together? You and the hockey guy?"

She looks past me when she says, "You might

say that. Married. Seven years. Not anymore. Not until he hooked up with—." She pauses. "I threw him out."

Inside of myself I'm nodding. I'm beginning to know exactly who he "hooked up with." I pull out the envelope with Jason's phone number on it and hand it to her. "That your cell?"

She looks down at it and nods.

"Not your husband's?"

She shakes her head and spits out the words, "He cheated once too often. Now tell me who you are and what you want."

I'm wondering, why did Jason put his wife's number on that Craig's List ad? "Your husband doesn't have a phone?" I ask.

She shakes her head. "Lost it. Months ago. Mostly he used mine. That's how much of a bum he was. Even his voice on the talk mail. I don't know how to change it—"

I nod, get up, walk out. The puzzle is all making sense now.

"Where you going?" she yells after me.

Before I leave, I take the hockey bag out of my trunk and leave it in the middle of her driveway. Let her deal with it. She had no idea her husband used her cell number on that Craig's List ad. At the mall, I pull the Nike shoe box out from where I stashed it under the passenger seat. I check. The gun is still there. I guess I forgot to tell you that part. I pulled the gun out of the hockey pants, cleaned it, wrapped it up in the blue scarf again, wrote Jason's address on a piece of paper and stuffed the whole works into this shoe box. Time to add a few more details to my note now.

Twenty minutes later I'm pulling out of the mall

and whistling. I have the music on loud and I'm singing along. And you can be glad you're not sitting beside me. I don't have the greatest voice.

A week later, the three of us are finishing our supper and on the news I hear, "Following an anonymous tip, the police have made an arrest in the slaying of student, Melissa Anders. Accused is Ruthann Meaghy who has also confessed to killing her husband—."

And then on the news I see that house, the place I went to, the place I walked around the inside of! The Tarzan lady!

I grab the remote and turn up the volume. I was right. Jason, well his real name, I learn, is Tony, was having an affair with Anders. RuthAnn, wife of seven years, found out, kicked him out. But that wasn't enough. She also killed Anders, stuffed the gun in her husband's hockey equipment so when it was found, he would be implicated. Well, it was me who found the bag, not the police that night. Tony wanted his equipment back and put an ad on Craig's List without RuthAnn knowing. And then when Tony discovered what RuthAnn did, he came after her. But big RuthAnn killed him first.

"Whoa, Marcie, whoa!"

"—Police found the murder weapon in a shoe box that had been left in a Postal Mail box in the Sherwood Mall along with a note leading the police directly to Meaghy."

I'm standing now, breathing deep, with the remote aimed at the screen.

"What's the matter, Jim?"

Then I'm smiling. Then I'm laughing hysterically. I grab Marcie around her waist and dance her around the kitchen.

I say, "How 'bout we pack up Olivia and take her over to Cheryl's and then you and me go out? Have I got a story to tell you!"

Marcie's looking at me strangely, and then she says, "You got any place in mind?"

"I was thinking maybe of Margaret's Pub, downtown."

Strange Faces

Weather Ladies

I've always been very protective of my sister.

Even when she started killing people at her work. And this time she wasn't even trying much to hide the evidence. I ran the bloodied scarf between my thumb and forefinger, and felt an emotion somewhere between fear and revulsion.

It was Monday morning and it befell me, as it does every Monday morning, to collect and wash her dirty laundry. I sat down on Corbin's bed and spread the awful thing across my lap. The blood on the scarf had dried to a dark reddish brown and there were bits of flesh and bone embedded into the fine fibers. Without even looking at the label I knew this was the Hermes scarf that had been used to choke to death Amanda Fish, the weather lady down at Cable 10 TV.

I threw it into the laundry basket and put a hand to my heart to quell a rising nausea. It would come clean, I decided. All of the blood and flesh would come out with a nice, hot bleach wash. Corbin's laundry has always been a challenge for me. My sister has this habit of stuffing her dirty clothes together in a heap in her hamper—good silk work blouses intermingled with her white socks and the sweaty tee-shirts she wears to the gym. No matter how many times I tell her about this, it falls on deaf ears.

I washed the scarf by itself four times, adding a capful of bleach to the final rinse. Just a capful. Too much and I would wash out all that lovely tangerine color.

I will protect my sister, I said to myself as I put the scarf in the dryer and set it to high heat. I always have. I always will. The three of us—Corbin, Mother and I have lived together for the past two years. When my husband died of an electrical shock in the bathtub two years ago I moved back with Corby and Mother. Mother was certainly glad when I did this. I think Mother has been slightly afraid of Corbin all these years. I can't say I blame her.

When I was fifteen Father died when he fell down the cellar steps. There is a whole other story there. A book, if you will. Please don't ask me to write about Father. There are two subjects that are closed to me—my dead husband and my dead father.

After I dried the scarf, I hot ironed it with a pressing cloth, folding it carefully in halves, then ironing that crease, and then into quarters and ironing it again. I slipped it into a Ziploc bag, scrunching out all of the air before sealing it. The scarf was still warm and the plastic crinkled into it. I took it upstairs to my bedroom and slid it between the mattress and box spring, reaching in as far as I could.

The dead Amanda Fish wore scarves. Every night when she did the channel 10 Weather, there was a scarf tied around her neck at some jaunty angle. At a time when other television ladies wore brooches and suits with their jackets revealing, in my opinion, far too much cleavage, Amanda Fish wore expensive scarves. It was her signature, Corbin said.

Amanda Fish had been choked so tightly that the pattern from the scarf and fibers had embedded itself into her neck. Can you imagine that? That was on the news.

Of course I didn't call the police when I found the scarf. Corbin is my sister, after all. Two months later, and the police still didn't have any leads. It wasn't even on the news anymore. Every so often I would check under my mattress for the scarf. Sometimes I pulled it out and had another look at it. At times the magnitude of the protection I was offering my sister frightened me.

Because after all of this, Corbin still didn't get the job. Two months after Amanda Fish was dead, my sister and I were watching the News and Weather at Six on 10. Corbin was on the couch cradling a bowl of popcorn between her pajama'd knees.

"You know, of course, it's not a real map behind her there." This was Corbin telling me.

"I know that," I said looking up from my sudoku. "Everybody knows that."

"I could do that." Corbin drew her long legs underneath her on the couch and placed the bowl beside her. "Anybody could."

Corbin works as a receptionist at channel 10, but is always talking about moving up, getting a job on air, doing the weather. She really wants to do the weather. There was a new weather lady now, Terry or Teresa Somebody who didn't wear scarves. She wore suits with silly pins on the lapels. Today she wore not one, but two butterfly pins high on her right shoulder.

"Don't you have to have special training for that?" I asked. "Like in meteorology or something?"

She guffawed. "That— " She emphasized the word that by poking a popcorn kernel in the air. "— Is a great misconception. It's all in the Teleprompter. It's easy. All you have to do is smile and look good. Unlike being an anchor, a weather lady has to have a good body, because you see so much of it. You want some popcorn? Help yourself." She passed me the bowl. I declined.

Terry or Teresa Somebody was indicating the jet-stream with a sweep of her hand, promising good weather for the weekend with a grin of white teeth. With a second low sweep she showed even more of herself.

My sister Corbin has a good body. It would be a good body for doing the weather. She's tall and muscular, but not cat-walk thin. She has shapely legs with well-developed calves which look good in short skirts. She plays a lot of sports. She has breasts that look like they were implanted, but they weren't.

She was eating her popcorn one kernel at a time to make it last longer. Corbin has all these tricks for keeping thin.

She continued, "And she makes good money, too."

Corbin is always talking about money, specifically about needing more money. She can't understand why Mother and I don't share more. I am quite well set up with my husband's life insurance and Mother has her money, of course from Father, but Corbin doesn't have much. She has student loans and expensive clothes, two things that don't mix.

Corbin has to learn to make her own way in the world and not spend all her money on Hermes scarves and suits and then throw them all together with the grimy, balled-up socks in the hamper and then expect me to make sense of it all.

"It's too bad you didn't get the job." I looked at her steadily.

"Maybe next time," she said shrugging.

"What?" I looked at her. "What did you say?"

"I said maybe next time."

"*What* next time?"

"I don't know. Terry won't be around long. To most of these people, this is just a stepping stone to a major network. If I get to do the weather, I'm going to stay here." Immediately she turned to me, "Hilly, I'm missing a scarf. Have you seen it?"

It wasn't lost on me—the fact that talking about the weather reminded her of that precise thing.

"A scarf?" My voice broke at the end.

"I spilled tomato bruschetta all over it."

I shook my head, unable to form words. I knew blood and body tissue when I saw it. Me, of all people.

She said, "I haven't seen it for a while, is all." Casual, so casual she was about it all.

I went back to my sudoku.

Corbin has never been a very good liar. Even when we were girls I could always catch her in a lie. Something about the way her eyes flicker and not look at you square on. She was doing that now, clasping and unclasping her fingers from the rim of the popcorn bowl, like she was very nervous, or very afraid.

A few days after this conversation, the second weather lady died. It turns out she was violently allergic to peanuts. Somehow she had ingested a peanut and immediately went into anaphylactic shock right there in the coffee room at Channel 10.

Again, I didn't know whether to confront her or not. I had spent late into the previous night cleaning up the mess of Corbin's fudge makings in the kitchen. She always leaves such messes. The kitchen is no different from her clothes hamper.

"It's for a party at work," she had said cheerfully. "For Teresa. She's taking the job permanently. We're all bringing stuff. I'm making my famous fudge."

"Your famous fudge. Good for you."

I was cleaning the house the day the second weather lady died. It needed to be spotless. Mother was due back from France. It seems as soon as she gets home she begins pouring through her Elderhostel catalogs and brochures to plan her next trip. Mother is on a mission. She wants to visit a hundred countries before she dies.

Corbin had come home from work that day with red eyes.

"Did you remember the groceries? I asked.

"Hilly, Teresa died today."

"What?" My broom in mid-sweep.

"Right in front of us all! We called 911 but it was too late. She even shot herself with her EpiPen, but it was too late. Oh Hilly, it was awful. She died in my arms."

I kept watching her, the way she was talking, the way her lips were forming words, but I saw something else behind them. There was no other way to describe what I saw in her eyes than glee. I remembered something else then, something from the night before. When she had been making that peanut butter fudge she had been humming.

I said, "Maybe you'll get the job now."

She looked at me. "How can you even say that?"

"Did you get the groceries?" I asked.

"Is that *all* you can think about? Is that all you can think about? Go out and get your own damn groceries!" She stomped off upstairs.

We would do without. Corbin knows I don't leave the house. She knows this. I sat down at the kitchen table and stared at the wall ahead of me, my hands balled together in my lap. I don't know how much time passed but soon she was back and sitting beside me.

"I'm sorry. I'm so sorry, Hilly. I don't know what came over me."

My gaze was still fixed on the wall. I didn't know how to answer her.

She tried again. "Are you okay, Hilly? It's not like the last time, is it? Do you want me to call Dr. Cochrane? I could get him to come here."

"I just need the groceries."

"Okay," she said touching my shoulder. "I'll run out and get them. I'll go now."

I gave her the list with a few last-minute corrections and she was off.

The next morning before she even got down the stairs for breakfast, I called to her. "Do you know where Mother is? She was supposed to be home last night." I tried to keep my lips from trembling. "But, her bed is empty. She never came home."

Corbin came into the kitchen. I was so stunned at the look of her that I momentarily forgot about Mother. My sister wore a pale pink suit that I'd never seen before and her hair was styled so that it fell to her shoulder in soft waves. She must've spent a long time with the flatiron to do that. Both of us have hard-to-tame curly hair. We get that from Mother.

"Your hair is different," I said.

"I'm doing the weather today." Her voice was strangely vacant. Corbin says that everything looks bigger on television—bodies, boobs, hair. "Just as a fill-in." She paused. "And Mother's in Belgium, by the way." She poured coffee into her travel mug.

"Belgium? How do you know that?" I asked. "We haven't gotten an email, a postcard. There's been nothing from her. I've been up all night with worry."

"She phoned," Corbin said matter-of-factly. "She called yesterday and with all that's happened with Terry, I forgot to mention it. She met some friends and they decided to go there."

"She called and told you this?" I was staring at her incredulously.

"Yes."

"I don't remember the phone ringing."

"It did, Hilly." There was an odd look on her face. "You just didn't hear it. Sometimes you don't hear things. You know that, right?"

I leaned into the door. It was warm in the room, but I started to shiver. "What did Mother say? What did she *say*?"

"That she'll be home in a couple of days and not to worry." Corbin ran a hand through her hair. She fiddled with one of her dangly earrings. Then, she trotted down the sidewalk in her high heels carrying her thermos and what looked like a new leather handbag. I watched her go and thought of something. A week or so ago, I'd needed a paperclip.

I couldn't find one in the usual places, so I had gone to Mother's roll top desk. I know where the key is. While searching for a paperclip I happened to notice that Mother's life insurance policy and bank books were missing. They had been right here and now they were gone. Had Corbin done this? Had Corbin *taken* them?

Because I was full of restless energy and needed to do something with my hands, I got down the lard and flour and rolling pin and the canned peaches. Quickly, I rolled out four pies and got them going in the oven.

Peach pies happily cooking, I went to my bedroom and pulled out the Ziploc bag. Maybe I shouldn't have washed it. Maybe I shouldn't protect my sister the way I do. I took it out, ran the silk through my fingers. The bleach had lightened the fabric somewhat, but that's what bleach and a hot water wash will do. Just for fun I tied it around my neck the way Amanda Fish wore it. I looked at myself in the mirror. Frowned. Then I pulled both ends tighter, tighter, and tighter until I was choking and coughing and gasping for breath. I pulled even tighter still until the fabric was in danger of tearing. So, I thought, this is what it feels like to be choked to death. Is this what happens to your eyes?

I put the scarf back in the bag and slid the back bag back under the mattress. It took me a while to stop coughing.

Downstairs, I took the peach pies out of the oven and turned the kitchen TV to the Noon News on Cable 10. Corbin looked nervous and I noticed that her hands weren't quite at the right places on the outlines of the map. I shook my head. And then I gasped, put a hand to my mouth.

I was staring, staring at the cellar door. Because I have not been down to the cellar since I moved back here, I keep it shut and dead-bolted. But now the lock was pulled back, and not only that, the door stood open an inch! I slunk back from the cellar door as if it were a living, breathing thing.

I sat down at the kitchen table and stayed there. I needed to talk with Corby about the door. She needed to explain to me why it was open. Our cellar is not a normal basement with a nice cement floor and windows, a place to store old furniture and out of season clothing. The ceiling is low and hung with cobwebs, and part of the floor in our cellar is dirt. The steps down are not like normal steps. They are very, very steep, practically as steep as a ladder. Before Father died, Mother used to store canning and potatoes down there. After he died no one went down there anymore.

I was still sitting at the table when Corbin clacked through the kitchen door in her high heels.

"Well, did you see it? Did you watch me?" She was cheerful, happy. "I kind of blew it at noon, but I was much better at six. Did you see me at six? I was so nervous at noon, because of Teresa and all, but I did much better at six. We're all trying to hang in. It's just so hard—" She looked at me. "Hilly?"

I hadn't seen her at six. I'd been sitting here. The whole afternoon I'd been sitting here. "What is it? She said. "Are you worried about Mother? Don't be. You know how she is—"

I stood to my feet and walked over to the cellar door. "This door was unlocked." My voice shook. "Open. Look at it!"

Corbin put her hand to her mouth and came over and stood beside me. "I know. I'm sorry. I was down there yesterday getting a shovel. I needed a shovel for something. I'm sorry. Has this upset you?"

I looked at her eyes, and all at once I knew what she had done. Mother had never gone to Belgium! Mother had probably not even gone to France. I knew where Mother was. Corby had killed her and buried her in the cellar. That was what the shovel business was all about.

She was standing right beside me now, both of us at the top of the steep steps. *Do it, Hilly. Don't think. Just do it!* I faced her and with one push, one unexpected shove, she was caught off guard and went stumbling down the stairs, screaming, calling my name, grabbing for handholds, looking up at me in astonishment.

You see, that was the problem with this old cellar. There had never been a handrail. I turned away and shut the door quickly behind me.

I sat back down where I'd been sitting all afternoon. I cut a piece of the now cooled peach pie and ate it with ice cream. Later, I made a pot of rose hips tea.

When night began to fall, I realized I couldn't leave her like that. She was my sister, after all. No, she would have to be buried next to Mother in the basement. It had to be done.

I opened the door. It was black down there. The light fixture had burned out long ago. I fumbled in the kitchen junk drawer for a flashlight, found one and shone it down the steps.

Corbin lay at the bottom in a jumbled heap of pink suit and red blood, her limbs akimbo, her head bent at an odd angle, eyes wide open. I started down the steps, one at a time, slowly, slowly, gripping the wall for support. Forcing myself, one step and then another and then another, until I was all the way down.

I was breathing hard and shaking as I dragged her body across the cold cement floor to the place where the dirt started. I needed something to dig with. Corby's shovel? I looked around and couldn't find it. Instead, I found a flat board and began digging. The dirt was as rigid as cement.

Over in the corner, next to the wall, the dirt was softer. But I couldn't dig there, could I? That was obviously where Corbin had buried Mother. What if I were to dig into soft flesh?

It took me well until morning to dig a hole deep enough. It was with great effort that I dragged her body to the hole and covered her over. Then, it was upstairs for the bleach bottle and mop. It was easier going down this the steps a second time, knowing that I would never have to come back down here again. Never.

By eight in the morning my work was done. I stepped out of my dirt encrusted clothing and put everything through a nice, hot bleach wash. Then I had a long soak in the tub. I even used some of Corbin's special bubble bath. I also used her body lotion when I finished. I'm prone to dry patches on my elbows, and this lotion would do nicely. Downstairs, I brewed another pot of rose hips and ate more pie.

At ten I called Channel 10. Corbin regrets to tell you that she has taken a job doing the weather out west. It came up rather suddenly. She got a call last night and left this morning on the first plane.

"Are you serious?"

"Yes."

"That's *unbelievable*."

"You know how Corbin is."

In the weeks that followed I felt fully justified, even when Amanda Fish's husband was arrested and admitted that he had killed his wife. Corbin must've been in on it. That's what it was. Corbin and Amanda's husband were having an affair. They must've done this together. Because, of course, they were still looking for the Hermes scarf. And then too, there was the little matter of the pinch of peanut butter that Corby had added to her batch of fudge which had killed Terry or Teresa Somebody.

Three weeks after I had been to the basement with Corbin, I was sitting at the kitchen table when I heard a noise at the door. I stared and stared as Mother walked in, bags slung over her shoulder, asking me for change for the cab driver and telling me that she was sorry, so sorry she couldn't email. She was away from Wi-Fi, "In the mountains," she added, but she had called Corbin. Did Hilary get the message? She was scurrying in with packages and boxes, her roller suitcase clicking on the hardwood. I didn't move.

"Hilary," she stopped. "What is it? You look like you've seen a ghost!"

"Corby's gone," I told her. "She took a job as a weather lady out west."

"Well, that's wonderful news, now isn't it? That's just what she wanted. Let me go up and unpack and then you can tell me all about it. Wow. Out West. Well, that explains why she's not answering her cell."

That night I pulled out the Ziploc bag. I pulled the scarf all the way out and lay the hideous thing across my lap. I picked it up and ran it through my fingers, staring long and hard at it. I gasped, groaned slightly and held my stomach. How could I have been so wrong about this? This was not a Hermes scarf at all! This one was cotton, cheap cotton, the kind you can buy in any dollar store and wrap around your forehead when you sweat in the gym. How had I not seen this?

I raced to the kitchen then. I found Corbin's recipe cards and began searching for the one for her famous fudge. I found it and then managed to find others. None of them, not one of them called for peanut butter. I rooted through the cupboards, pulling out pots, bowls, recipe cards, containers of lard, cookbooks. Corbin hated peanut butter. Even as a girl, she hated it. We didn't even have any peanut butter. We never buy peanut butter. Corby hates peanut butter. How could I have not remembered this?

I heard a noise and looked to the doorway. Mother was standing there in her pink dressing gown.

"We don't have any peanut butter," I exclaimed, almost shrieking, but I couldn't get my voice to be any quieter. "There's none in the house! She always hated peanut butter! She never would have baked anything with peanut butter in it! Not a thing!"

Mother didn't say anything. She merely approached me, her hands reaching toward me. "Hilary?"

I backed away from her.

She stopped and a look crossed her face. "Where is Corbin?" She asked steadily. "Where is your sister?"

My teeth began to chatter and I couldn't keep my gaze from drifting to the cellar door. She saw where I was looking and said, "Where is she?"

She walked toward the open cellar door and looked down. Yes. It was open. I had not closed and locked it after all. "Oh Hilary," she said. "What have you done? What have you done *now*?"

I followed her, stood right behind her. *Don't think Hilly! Just do it!*

Strange Faces

A Small Season of Magic

You are asking for margarine today. Over and over you are saying the word "margarine," or something that sounds like margarine. I'm not sure. Your mouth slurs around the vowels.

"Margarine?" I ask. "You want margarine? Instead of butter?"

You nod. Then shake your head. Your lips move. I lean in closer and we repeat the conversation. This is what happens lately. We talk around things. We go over things and over things and I'm never quite sure what you're getting at. I want to stop this discussion before it upsets you. I say the word one more time. "Margarine?" I pronounce it carefully, cautiously and look into your eyes.

You nod. "Margarine."

This is odd for you. You grew up on butter and have always disdained the use of foods like margarine.

"For lunch?" you say.

"Okay."

Somewhere a clock is chiming the time. There is a loose brown thread on the cuff of your sweater and you study it with great intensity. I take off my glasses, fold them and lay them across my lap. One of the frame arms is slightly askew and subconsciously I rub my finger and thumb across the bent part. You did this to my frames yesterday when you yanked them from my face and flung them hard into the wall.

You lean forward in the La-Z-Boy, one cotton pant-leg skewed around your thigh. I bend to straighten it, and you swat my hand away as you would a bug. My glasses fall to the floor. I sigh. I am trying not to take these things personally, yet it stings. I can't help it. I'm your wife and human in all of this. You go back to fiddling with your sweater cuff and mumbling.

"Okay," I say bending down for my glasses to put them back on. "I will get some margarine. How about a sandwich? Would you like a sandwich? A sandwich with margarine on it? That's what I'll go and get."

"Not margarine, exactly," you say. "I can't remember what."

You grope around the side table with the fingers of one hand searching for something.

"My glasses," you say.

I reach for them and place them on your face. You take the instruments off and look down at them as if you have no idea what they are for. This deeply saddens me. For more than sixty years you meticulously fitted eyes with glasses, all sorts of eyes and all sorts of glasses. You were a perfectionist and your patients knew it. And now this—

"And a McRib from McDonald's?" you add. I catch a glimpse of something light and humorous behind your pale, filmy eyes, your words are focused and lucid and clear. Some days you seem fine and perfect, your speech not slurred at all. And then in the next minute you are up and wandering through the rooms of our house looking for a specific square piece of cheddar or a tin of cocoa or the tea kettle you had in your office fifty years ago.

"I don't think McDonald's makes McRibs anymore," I tell you. "Would you like a Big Mac instead?" I ask. I keep my voice as light as I can. "I could try to get one with extra cheese? Maybe even extra meat? And margarine," I add as an afterthought. This last word seems to upset you.

The empty look is back on your face again, that look that erases all memories of our entire life together, the whole fifty-six years of our marriage. I remember that you are not you anymore. You are you, but with a brain that is slowly coming apart, falling away, piece by piece.

The nurse has told me that your past will become your present and that your present will be lost. When this happens, childhood memories will become more and more your present reality. As you regress, you will remember with perfect clarity to when you were twenty-five, twenty, eighteen.

I don't want to tell the nurse this, but this is exactly what I am waiting for.

I need for you to finally tell me about that time, the time before we were together when we were both so young—children really.

The time of the magic.

The water is running in the kitchen. Marty is washing out pots. I pat your hand. "I'll be back soon," I tell you. I go into the kitchen and tell Marty that I'm heading out to look for a McRib sandwich, and that nothing else will quite do. I roll my eyes when I say this. I add that you are somewhat fixated on margarine and I really don't know why.

She tells me to take my time. You and she will be quite all right here by yourselves. "Stop in and get yourself a coffee if you want. Take some time for yourself."

Marty is our daughter, our only child. She and her small granddaughter live with us here. The girl's mother, my own granddaughter, has gone off to somewhere nobody knows. But that whole episode is for another story, not this one. Although, I grieve for Marty, it is for Anna, my great-granddaughter that I need for you to tell me the secrets.

Zipping up my fleece jacket, I ask, "How is Anna today?"

Marty shrugs, looks away, dries her hands on a dish towel. "Now the school wants to meet with me. The principal. I just don't know if it's worth it." She shakes her head, looks lost. "I can't help thinking that all this intervention just seems to add to it somehow, ya know?"

I nod. I know. Anna is small. That's why the kids pick on her. I know what that's like. My bullying happened a long time ago when teachers and parents didn't intervene so much, when bullying was considered something to be worked out between kids. It didn't take the national stage with programs and slogans and posters. Often victims were blamed for not standing up for themselves. I know I was.

Back then, telling your teacher was considered tattling, and invariably made things worse. Teachers then, I am convinced, really didn't know what to do when a child complained of being picked on. And sometimes, some horrible and unimaginable times, it was the teachers themselves who did the bullying, teachers like Miss Wagoner, in her prim plaid skirts and perfectly pin-curled hair. It was this teacher who would make me stand at my desk, and stand there and stand there until I gave the correct answers to the sums on the board.

"This one's easy," she would say to me, loud enough so that the whole class heard. "This one is so easy even you should have no trouble with it—"

More titters.

When I couldn't, when from nerves or shyness my eyes blurred and my brain couldn't formulate the answers, she would scowl at me until I couldn't hold back the tears. Only then would she order me to sit.

"Sit! Sit down now! Get some sense into you! How old are you anyway!"

As I slunk into my seat, I would hear the sniggers of all my classmates. As a final dig, she would mutter something under her breath that I heard, that we all heard. "You'd think with those glasses of hers, she'd be able to see—"

Now, as I walk out the kitchen door, Marty says to me, "Yesterday a couple of the kids took her glasses."

I stop. *What*? "What did you say?"

"They took her glasses. A teacher got them back though. They were all right, not broken or anything."

"Her *glasses*?"

"Yes." Marty is eyeing me strangely. I have never told her about the magic. In all of these years I have never told anyone about the magic. And I need to. I know that. I need to before you and I are both gone.

"Well," I say trying to compose myself, "I'm glad

they weren't broken. That's good, at least."

I rush outside to my car, my knees trembling. I need to think. Yesterday it was you who tore my glasses from my face and flung them away from me. "Take them off. Leave them off," you yelled. And now Anna's classmates had taken hers!

You have been grabbing at my glasses more and more and this has me wondering how much you remember about the glasses.

When Marty told the nurse that you had grabbed for my glasses, she sighed and said that bully behaviors are a side effect of the disease's progression. Can you imagine? A disease where bullying is a side effect? Not nausea or vomiting, but bullying? It's odd to me and so very heartbreaking that you, who once saved me from the bullies, are now a bully yourself. Do you know this? Do you even see the irony in all of this?

I drive to three McDonald's and of course no one sells McRibs. A tired looking fat girl at the third McDonald said they haven't sold them in years. I buy two Big Macs instead, one for you and one for later. You and I normally shunned such food, but what harm can it do now? Besides, by the time I get home you will probably have changed your mind.

I count out my change, catching a glimpse of myself in the glass behind the counter. I hardly recognize that haggard, thin-lipped, raggedy-haired, droopy-eyed face with the crooked glasses. When did this happen to me that I became so old, my face so exhausted?

I carry the little white bag out to the car and place it on the passenger seat beside me. I am sitting in the car in the McDonald's parking lot and I cannot think to move, to back out, to drive home. I take off my glasses and rub my leaky eyes. I finger one of the earpieces and sit there. I should go and get them straightened. I don't care that there are people waiting to get my parking space in this busy place. I don't care. I sit there.

***

I am thirteen again and the terrible and wonderful thing is about to happen to me. When I was little, like Anna, my glasses were as thick as the bottom of Coke bottles. Young people today neither understand what a Coke bottle is or that glasses can actually look like them. These days Coke comes in cans and eyeglass lenses are made of feather-weight plastic. I have lived with you and lived through all the technological changes in eyeglasses. You embraced every change with eagerness and never stopped upgrading your knowledge and the equipment in your clinic.

Back in school a lot of the kids laughed at me, but there were three in particular who took to bullying me in a serious way. They were my age, but a whole lot bigger than I could ever hope to be. The three of them followed me home each day, staying a few feet behind me taunting me, calling me names. I tried to ignore them, but they were always there. My father said the problem was that I didn't stand up for myself. All I needed to do, according to him, was to turn around and tell them in my biggest voice to leave me alone and not come back. I couldn't do this. Of course I couldn't do this. That would make them laugh at me more. I knew this.

I had two routes to get home from school. I could stay on the sidewalk all the way around to my street, and then backtrack to my house. Or, I could take a short cut through the woods. The path cut the trek by half, but the woods were a fearful place to us kids. It was the place where my brother and I would run through to the very end, sure we were being chased by boogie men or hobos. There were animals in the woods, too. Sometimes at night we could hear them.

And it was in the woods, where on that day, the awful thing happened; the terrible, awful, magical thing.

Even though I was walking by myself, I decided to take the path. I was sure I would be okay. Nothing could happen on such a sunny day like this, could it? Besides, since I hadn't seen my taunters anywhere after school, I was sure they were long gone.

They weren't.

Just ahead where the path turns to the right, there they were, jostling each other and laughing. They ignored me. They didn't see me? Maybe I was in luck. I hung back, turned around and looked behind me. I should go back the other way. But maybe it would be okay. There was only a little more of the path before it came out to the street.

They slowed. I slowed. The three of them were playfully shoving each other and laughing. I hugged my book bag a little closer to my chest and forced myself to breathe normally as I put one foot in front of the other.

I was almost to the bend in the path when they turned as one and faced me. They were grinning and grinning. They'd known I was there, pathetically creeping along behind.

"Whatcha doing shrimpy four-eyes?" the Biggest Big Girl said.

I ignored them, turned and began walking back

the other way.

"Running back to the teachers to tattle?" the Middle Big Girl asked.

"Hey four-eyes!" the Smallest Big Girl said. "We're talking to you."

I held my book bag tightly and kept going.

The Big Girl's voice was too close when she said, "We're talking to you, bug."

"Yeah you, bug!"

"Lady bug, lady bug fly away home."

My knees began to wobble. I would never make it out. They were close. Too close.

"Whatcha got in your bag, little girl?" The Biggest Big Girl reached out and jabbed my shoulder with her hand.

I kept my head down and put one foot in front of the other. Walk faster. *Walk faster*. Leave me alone. *Leave me alone*.

"We're talking to you, shrimp," the Middle Girl added.

"Yeah. What's in your book bag?"

"Um," I said. "My b-books."

"Oh, your b-books," said the Smallest Big Girl.

"Can we see your b-books?" the Middle Girl asked.

I shook my head, close to tears. Just a few more steps. Surely they wouldn't keep this up when we were back on the main road.

The Biggest Big Girl said, "Well, if you're not going to show us your b-books, I guess we'll have to come and see your b-books ourselves."

The smallest one grabbed my book bag from me. The movement was so fast and so sudden that I lost my grip on it. She opened it up and dumped the contents on the dirt path. There went my pencils and books and papers. The middle girl kicked my papers further. My arithmetic primer got opened and spread into a mud puddle. I stifled a sob. Now Miss Wagoner would kill me for sure!

When I bent to retrieve them, the big girl jabbed me hard in the side. With a gasp and a groan, I fell onto my face on the rooty, stony ground. My glasses fell off and the smallest one kicked them away from my grasp. Then the big one stepped on them grinding them into the dirt. My glasses!

By this time I was sobbing, which only ignited them further. My side hurt and my elbows were all skinned, my face was bloody and I couldn't see, and still they stood around me taunting me, jabbing at me with their feet, battering me with their elbows, their fists. When I attempted to rise, the biggest one slugged me and I fell back onto my head. Hard.

I don't remember what happened after that. They must have fled, because when I opened my eyes I was alone and it was darker. I rose; shaky, uncertain, and gathered my dirty papers and my ruined glasses, and headed home.

Because I was "blind as a bat" as my mother was fond of saying, she took me in hand to Dr. Peterson's right that afternoon to get a new lens made for my glasses. My mother was furious. First of all, I was an hour late and she was "worried sick" and secondly, I was a mess. When I tried to explain through my tears what happened, she grabbed my shoulder and said I should have been "more careful." I should have taken the sidewalk home. How many times had she told me this, and yet I insisted on walking through the woods? Well, now you see what happens. This is what comes of it.

The glass in both lenses was crushed and the

frames were bent, but my mother thought that Dr. Peterson might be able to fix them. We weren't in a "financial position" she said, to get a complete new set of frames and glasses.

That's where the two of us met. You were working in the office for the doctor who gave me my temporary glasses.

It would be many more years before you and I would meet again, and when we did, I would be eighteen and you would be twenty-six. I would be out with my parents and my aunt at a hotel restaurant. When I spied you in the doorway then, I gasped, jumped up, and without explanation I began to make my way quickly to where you were standing at the door. Through the years, I think I had almost convinced myself that you weren't real. So when I saw you, I knew I had to talk to you. I had to.

"Hey!" I called. I pushed past occupied tables, bumped into chairs, elbowed my way past startled people. "Hello! Hey!"

By now you'd turned toward me. A woman in a red coat and fur collar was holding tightly to your arm.

"Hello! Hey! Hello!" I was breathless when I finally had your attention. "I don't know if you, um, if you remember me—" I paused to catch my breath. "But I remember you. I was thirteen, I'm eighteen now, and you were working for Dr. Seegam and I was there. And—and—I just wanted, um, I just wanted to say thank you for everything you did for me that day. And if you see Dr. Seegam can you thank him, too? I never got the chance."

You were smiling a little when you said, not unkindly, "I'm sorry? What did you say the name was? Seegam? Sorry, I'm afraid I don't know anyone by that name. Perhaps you have me mixed up with someone else?" The woman in fur held more firmly to your arm and frowned at me and at the commotion I'd caused in the busy restaurant.

"You have to remember me!" I was desperate. "Don't you? At all? Even a little? I will never forget you! I would recognize you anywhere! I saw you in the doorway and knew right away it was you. How can you not remember?"

By this time my mother and spinster aunt were there and scowling at me. I had a picture of what I must have looked like—hair coming out of its pins, out of breath, lipstick probably worn off during the meal, shiny face. Everyone, in fact, was glowering at me except for you. In contrast, you seemed amused by it all.

My mother grabbed hold of my arm, but I wrenched it away. I had more to say. "How can you not remember?" She grabbed hold again, harder this time and forced me away. But when I looked back, you winked at me.

Years before, you had winked at me in just that same way. You had cleaned up my glasses with a shimmery cloth, and before giving them to me, you winked. Over the years I have grown to know and love that wink so well.

But on that day, that terrible day when I was thirteen, all I was was scared. My mother and I took the bus to the eye doctors, me complete with skinned knees, bruised face, broken glasses and all. Dr. Peterson told my mother that they could fix my glasses, but that it would be several weeks before they could get to them. The lab, which was located behind the office, was backed up with orders.

"Completely backed up," he said, his hands spread out. "So sorry."

I had looked up at him and tried not to cry. For two weeks I would have no glasses. That meant I wouldn't be able to see the board. And tomorrow was the arithmetic test. Miss Wagoner wouldn't care, as if she needed another excuse to make fun of me in front of the whole class. I kind of wandered away a bit from where my mother and Dr. Peterson and the nurse were talking earnestly and fingering my bent frames. I was looking longingly at the sets of new eyeglass frames along one wall, wishing we were "in a financial position" to get new ones. I was trying not to cry.

"You had a bit of a run in there didn't you?" Another doctor, a small man, was standing beside me. He wore a white doctor coat which hung on his shoulders like it was a bit too big for him. He was older than Dr. Peterson and his white head looked like a patch of dandelions gone to seed.

I nodded.

With a small bow he said, "Well, I might may be able to help you. I'm helping Dr. Peterson today and I have a lot of temporary glasses for girls who can't see the numbers on the board."

I looked at him.

"And you've got an arithmetic test tomorrow don't you? You're going to certainly need some temporary glasses in that case."

How did he know that? That was the trouble with my mother, she blabbed way too much about everything.

He paused, put a forefinger under his chin in a rather dramatic way and said, "I think we might have a way to solve your problem. Come on back with me."

I looked around for my mother but the three of them, she and Dr. Peterson and the nurse were still in conversation. When he saw my hesitation he said, "The nurse will direct your mother down to my office in a minute. You might as well get started. Come on back and you can begin looking at some of the glasses I have."

"Okay."

I followed him down the hall, which seemed to go on forever. I don't remember it being quite this long. Maybe they built onto it since my last time here. That was my thought as I followed the little man in the oversized lab coat. He was quite chatty and told me that his name was Dr. Seegam, and that he sometimes came in and helped Dr. Peterson with young people who had broken glasses, and had three big girls who bullied them. I looked up at him. Had my mother told him everything?

At the very end of the hall, I followed him into a perfectly square room with a ceiling so high I couldn't see to the top of it without my glasses.

You were in that room. You were sitting at one of two dusty card tables. Your hair was red and short and curly and you wore an impossibly bright green vest. You smiled at me. And winked.

I stared. At you. At the tables. At the walls. Especially at the walls. As far up as my weak eyes could see were shelves and shelves of boxes which were the size and shape of shoeboxes with numbers and lettering and labels taped haphazardly on the faces of them.

Everything in the room had a fine sheen of dust including Dr. Seegam. A sprinkling of gray soot lay on his shoulders like he had been hanging in a dingy closet. Even you were covered in dust.

Dr. Seegam leaned down and whispered a few words to you. You nodded. There were several boxes of loose eyeglasses on your table and you were going through them, sorting them and cleaning them with a variety of neon colored cloths, a different color for each set of glasses. I thought this was odd and kept watching. After each pair of glasses was cleaned, you placed them back into boxes. Your vest had many pockets which contained all of your colored cleaning cloths.

"That's my assistant," Dr. Seegam said. "He's in his second year of optometry school." I don't think he mentioned your name. Or if he did so, I didn't catch it. Probably, I was too overwhelmed.

As instructed I sat down at the other table which was rickety and old and empty except for a gilded hand mirror. I picked it up, surprised at its heft. I had seen one like this at my grandmother's dressing table, all heavy and intricately designed.

The room had a movable ladder on wheels which rode along the high walls. Dr. Seegam climbed this ladder to the very top. He fingered a few of the dusty boxes, frowned, moved the ladder a bit more and then picked up another box and said, "Ah. This should do. This should do quite nicely." He climbed down the ladder, the box firmly under his arm.

There was a twinkle in his eye when he plunked the shoebox full of glasses down onto the table in front of me. These weren't new glasses all arranged neatly lined up in their own individual cases, but loose glasses all jumbled together. And like everything in the room, they were covered liberally with dust. My mother would have a fit here, I was sure. I stared doubtfully into the contents of the box.

"It's okay," he told me. "Choose a pair. My assistant hasn't gotten to cleaning these ones yet. But no matter, pick the pair you like and I'll get him to shine them up all nice and clean for you."

Gingerly, I reached into the box and pulled out a pair of glasses from the bottom. I expected them to be old and grimy and weird, and for an old lady, but as soon as I picked them up they felt warm in my hands. I blew away a bit of the dust and saw that these were the most beautiful frames I'd ever seen. They were a shimmery pale blue, a blue that was sort of the sky and sort of the sea. But neither. And better.

"Those?" he said.

I nodded, swallowed. "They look nice," I said. I had my doubts I'd be able to see through them. Didn't they have to get lots of measurements and make them in a lab? Plus, the glass in these seemed so thin, thinner than any window I had ever looked through.

He took them from me, and said, "We'll have to get these specially cleaned up for you. It's arithmetic you're having a special problem with, right?" When I nodded, he said to you, "That would be the red cloth, then."

"Red cloth?" you asked.

"Yes. Not the orange-red or the maroon-red, but the bright red. The true red. There are many different shades of red."

"Okay. Got it," you said.

He turned to me. "And three big girl bullies?"

I nodded again.

"Bullies?" you said to Dr. Seegam. You reached into your pockets and pulled out a black cloth as shimmery as patent leather.

Dr. Seegam shook his head rather vigorously. As he did so flecks of what looked like dandruff floated around him. "No, no, no. Not that one. Not the black one. Three big girl bullies. That one's for small boy bullies, not three big girl bullies. If you use that cloth it will be no help at all. No help at all. Use the brown cloth in your topmost right pocket."

"Okay, boss."

You took it out and began shining them first with the red cloth and then with the brown. I watched entranced, because something funny was happening. Dust particles flew off the glasses in every direction, but instead of behaving like normal dust, this dust seemed to have a life of its own. It would hover in the air a bit and then move sideways attaching itself to other objects. I watched, entranced.

When the glasses were cleaned, you handed them to Dr. Seegam. He turned them every which way and then took out a silver cloth from his coat pocket and shined the entire glasses, including the frames and the arms and the nose piece. He did this several times, examining them in the light and shining again and again until he was satisfied.

He placed them on my face with gentle fingers.

The first thing I noticed was that I barely felt them on my face. Part of what I hate about glasses is that they're so heavy. They hurt my ears, my nose and they're always falling off. Sometimes I get these big red marks on my nose from where they press against. And there are times that the back of my ears hurt so much it's like I have a really bad headache.

The second thing I realized was that I could see perfectly. Perfectly. I could see every outline of every box. I could read what was on every one of them, even the ones on the topmost shelves. I saw that they were categorized with labels like, *Two Boy Bullies, Special Problems With Sums, Girl Bullies, Trouble With Piano Lessons, Special Problems With Teachers, Girls Who Are Eight,* and on and on the labels went.

I stared, transfixed at everything. And the dust? This wasn't dust. This looked like living particles of gold. I reached my hand in front of me and looked at it for several seconds. My fingernails shimmered. Dust particles settled on my fingers like tiny diamonds which stayed for a minute before taking off. All of the formerly dusty shelves shimmered as if they were alive.

"Are they fairies?" I asked. You and Dr. Seegam smiled at me.

Dr. Seegam held the mirror up in front of me and I looked at my reflection. I was astonished. With these glasses nobody would ever call me four eyes. These were less like glasses and more like diamond jewelry. Even my hair, dull and dishwater blonde shimmered in the mirror.

"Wow!" was all I said.

He looked over at you then, a wide smile on his wizened face. "I think she likes them. I really think she likes them."

You regarded me for a moment and then you spoke, words I would always remember. "They look nice. They make you look very pretty."

I felt myself blushing and hoped it didn't show.

I said, "These work good. Do you think I could just have these? I mean, instead of getting my old ones fixed? Can you ask my mother? Dr. Peterson? Are they expensive?" But I knew without asking that this was the case. If we weren't "in a financial position" to buy ordinary glasses, I was sure these would be completely out of the question.

For a little while Dr. Seegam looked at me sort of sadly. Maybe he was considering my request, but then he said with a shake of his head, "I'm afraid not. We need these for other girls who come in with broken glasses from bullies. These will work for you until your old ones are fixed. The only way I can loan you these is if you promise to bring them back."

"I will."

"Do you promise?"

"I promise."

You were looking at me and grinning. You still wear that same grin. In all the years of our lives together, I have never grown tired of your grin and your red hair and your wink. But on that day your hair shimmered like strawberry gold. And from here I could see that your eyes glimmered. They were so blue, like the color of my new glasses.

"Well," Dr. Seegam said. "Maybe it's time to go. Your mother and Dr. Peterson will be waiting out front."

It was you who escorted me down the hall where my mother was standing in the reception room, impatiently tapping her foot.

"Where have you been?" she asked.

"I was getting glasses."

"Maybe she was in the ladies' room," the nurse offered. "Is that where you were, honey?"

"No. I told you—" I pointed to my eyes. "I got these."

"You said she had a fall?" Dr. Peterson was ignoring me as he and my mother talked.

"—And hit her head," my mother said.

"Well," he said. "I wouldn't worry too much,

unless she starts exhibiting other symptoms like nausea or vomiting. She might seem a little confused for a while. And we're so sorry about the long wait for the glasses. We'll get them fixed as soon as we can. I'll put a priority on them. I hope she can manage in school."

"I told you—" I said trying to get their attention. "I have these! I can see perfectly! The doctor in the back—" I pointed, but no one was listening.

"I could write a note to the school," the nurse said.

My mother nodded. "That would be helpful."

They were all talking above me and around me, but not to me. But it suddenly didn't matter. I was looking around the reception area. Things had never been so bright, so clear. There were rainbows everywhere. Rainbows glinted off the walls displaying eyeglass frames. Rainbows ran across the ceiling and onto the light fixtures, and even across the nurse's face. It looked so funny it made me laugh. "Rainbows!" I said.

"It's time to go," my mother said. "Thank you Dr. Peterson, for all your help."

When I turned to say goodbye, you were gone.

***

I have finally put the car in reverse and I am backing out of the McDonald's parking place. I don't want the magic to die with you. Anna needs the magic of the glasses. So many children need the magic. If only I could unlock it from your brain. If only you would talk about it.

A guy behind me, big guy, young, loud music from his truck, gives me the finger as I back out. I guess he doesn't appreciate an old lady sitting here for so long, taking up prime McDonald's real estate. "I can stay here as long as I want," I want to yell at him. "I have a husband at home who is dying. Soon it will be you. And you will be surprised at how quickly it comes."

But his gesture infuses me with something else. I remember back to the glasses. I look at him again and he is nothing but a diminutive little man, hair sprouting out of a pink scalp, barely able to peer over the steering wheel of his humongous truck with its roaring hip hop.

***

Rainbows werc everywhere on the way home from the doctor's on the bus that day. I remarked about this to my mother who merely sighed.

"But don't you see them? A double rainbow is supposed to be good luck, right? Over there. There are like a million double rainbows. And they go on forever and ever into the sky. And look right ahead out the front of the bus. There's a triple rainbow. I've never seen a triple rainbow before."

My mother frowned and went back to her magazine.

I went on, "I think it's because everything is so shimmery because of the rain. The rain is so pretty. Don't you think?"

"It's not raining." She turned to me. "Are you all right? Does your tummy hurt?"

I looked straight ahead and was a bit confused. Yes, it was raining. That was rain out there. The raindrops looked like little diamonds as they hit the big front windshield of the bus in slow motion and then split into a million satiny pieces. Why was she telling me it wasn't raining when it was? I asked my mother this and she shook her head and said to me rather pointedly, "I think you need to be less focused on this imaginary rain and more on your arithmetic test tomorrow. Did you bring your books with you? You could study on the bus you know." And then she added, "Don't forget to take the note to school tomorrow."

"It's okay." I pointed at my eyes. "I don't need a note."

I leaned my head into the seat back. I had my numbers books with me. I'd managed to wipe off most of the mud, but how can you study for something when you don't understand it in the first place? And when your teacher doesn't even want to help you? Every time I went to Miss Wagoner for extra help it seemed like she made fun of me. All she kept saying was that I needed to pay better attention in class. Like all the other students. I opened up my book, but my attention was on the upholstery on the bus seat ahead of me. It was intricate and full of designs and patterns. It looked like expensive carpet. I reached forward to trace the colorful whorls with my fingers, and my mother reached for my hands.

"Dirty," she said. "Don't touch that."

But when she grabbed my hand to move it away, my fingers left traces of pink sparkles in the air. And so for the rest of the trip home I moved my fingers around in front of my face, looking at the spirals of pink and gold that they left in the air while my worried mother licked her lips and watched me.

No one at home seemed as enthralled about my new glasses as I was, not my father, not my mother, not my brother. In the kitchen I could hear my mother talking quietly and worriedly to my father. "I don't know what's the matter with her. She's seeing things now."

"What things?"

"Rainbows, specifically. And rain."

"Ah, I wouldn't worry too much. You know how she is."

"Maybe those girls really did hurt her. Maybe the fall on her head was worse than we thought. Do you think we need to take her to the doctor's?"

"What did Dr. Peterson say?"

"He said to make sure she gets rest and to watch for signs of nausea and vomiting."

"Well, we'll do that then."

Then they said something I couldn't hear, finally my father's voice, "That girl needs to learn to stand up for herself. There are bullies everywhere in life. If she doesn't learn it now she'll just have to learn it later. Maybe this is a good lesson for her. Maybe this will all be for the best."

***

In the ensuing years I've looked up the name Dr. Seegam on every scrap of paper that I could find in your office, every bill, every bit of correspondence, every letter that came in. Sometimes I would sneak in at night and go through all of your files, every one. I never found a thing.

When we got the Internet, I searched everywhere. I have spent hours on the computer, and I never found any reference to a Dr. Seegam who was an optometrist back in the forties. I tried all sorts of spellings. Nothing. Nothing. And when I would ask you, all you would say was, "You should write it all down." And then you would wink at me.

"Maybe I will someday. Maybe I just will."

I like to think it was the magic which brought the two of us together. Because a week after I'd chased you down in the restaurant you were standing at my door. My mother came to my room late one afternoon and said, "There is a young man downstairs to see you."

I was shocked when I came down and it was you. You introduced yourself, said you had been so impressed with the way I ran up to you in the restaurant, "so full of spunk," you said, that you had to find me. You had asked around, looked me up, "And here I am," you said.

"Here you are," I said.

Six months later we were married, the girl in the red coat and fur collar long forgotten.

But never, never in fifty-seven years of marriage have you ever admitted or spoken about your association with Dr. Seegam and by default me. But I like to think that you came to the door because all of it was true. All of it is true.

***

I went to my room that first night with my temporary glasses, but I didn't really open my books at all. I kept being distracted by how everything in my room shimmered and shook. I went over to my wall and put my hand on its warm surface, my fingers still exuding pink glitter when I moved them about.

When I took off my glasses, everything returned to normal. I sat down on my bed and studied them wondering if there was something embedded in the glass that made rainbows appear everywhere, like a kaleidoscope. I couldn't find a thing.

When it was supper time I went downstairs and

looked at the food on my plate for a long time before I picked up my fork. The mashed potatoes looked golden. The peas were individually formed and the most perfect shade of green.

My father pointed with his fork. "You better eat up."

"It's like eating gold," I said, and my parents looked at each other.

Later, it was my turn to do dishes. When I put my fingers in the water they felt like they were encased in soft satin. It was velvety and strange and silky and milky and not like dish water at all. I could have stayed at the sink all night.

I have to admit I really didn't get very much studying done that night. I would open a book and all the letters and numbers would dance on the pages like they were alive. If I thought really hard, if I concentrated, they would be still but if I let my eyes skim the surface, they danced. I even thought I heard music although I'm sure that must have been my imagination. Because how can music come from a kaleidoscope?

In a little while my mother came in and told me it was time for me to think about getting to bed. In bed, I was reluctant to take these glasses off. I could see Orion and the Big Dipper on my ceiling. And there was the Milky Way. It was like I was seeing right through my ceiling and out onto the perfect night sky.

When I was little my grandmother showed me all the stars as we lay covered in a blanket out on the farm where everything is dark. It was as if we were on her porch and she was pointing them all out to me. The funny thing was, as I looked at the stars and constellations, I remembered what she told me.

I remembered all of their names.

I heard a noise, slight at first. I got up and went to my window. In the far distance and over the mountains someone was setting off fireworks. They kept exploding in the sky while I watched.

Later, much later I fell asleep with my glasses on. My dreams were full of waterfalls and rainbows, shimmering sunlit paths, constellations and fireworks.

The following day at school I wanted everyone to admire my new glasses which I decided were the color of summer rain. But people jostled me and ignored me like they always did. The Big Girls who had punched me on the path the day before were standing at the classroom door and eyeing me warily.

When I looked at them, something strange happened. The Biggest Big Girl, the one with the brown curls, grew smaller, bit by bit in front of me until she came to my waist. Her voice got tinier, too, tinier and tinnier. It was like she was talking to me from inside a garbage can. The Medium Big Girl with the skinny nose grew bonier and scragglier until she looked like a witch, her mouth a red slash across the bottom of her face. The Little Big Girl, the one with the black hair shrank before my eyes until she resembled a bloated Cockroach shaking on the ground. All I could do was stare and stare. And then I began to laugh. I couldn't help myself. I laughed.

"What are you laughing at, bug?" the Little Big Girl said in her high, squeaky voice.

"You," I said. "And I'm not the bug, you are."

"What are you talking about? What are you talking about?" Her little cockroach body shivered and shook, but I simply laughed more. The three of them looked so funny.

"What are you laughing at now?" the Middle Girl said.

"At you," I said. "I'm bigger than you are now, in case you hadn't noticed. I'm bigger than all of you put together."

When I walked past, I took off my glasses and looked back at them.They were the same as always, big and scary and looking at me with hate in their eyes. I quickly put my glasses back on and they all huddled together like a pack of small rodents. They skulked away, whimpering and giving me scared little backward glances.

In arithmetic class I stopped in the door and stared at Miss Wagoner. There were spots all over her face, and her hair, usually arranged so perfectly, was in disarray. Every time she moved, bobby pins fell out. Her blouse was coming untucked from her carefully pleated skirt. Her whole outfit looked like it all needed ironing. I tried not to stare at her.

I glanced around, but no one else was sniggering at her behind their hands.

I sat down. The math problems were written on the board in white chalk. We were instructed to take a clean sheet of paper and write down the questions and then our answers making sure to show all our work. I tore out a couple of pieces of plain notebook paper and wrote my name on the top right with shimmery silver ink. Or at least that's the way the pencil lead looked to me. The numbers on the board were very clear. So that was good.

And then I noticed something. Next to the chalk problems and written in gold were more numbers and problems.

"Are there any questions?" Miss Wagoner said.

I looked around me. Everyone was writing, their heads bent low over their papers.

The teacher stared at me. "You can get to work any time now."

I stood up beside my desk.

"Yes? You have a question?"

"Miss Wagoner, what's the writing in yellow?"

"Excuse me?" A couple of bobby pins from her hair fell to floor. She didn't seem to notice.

"Right next to the problems. Numbers. In yellow. They're pretty faint but I can still see them." I pointed.

She turned and looked at the board, then back at me. Her blouse was completely untucked now, and the frilly end of her slip was showing at the side of her skirt. She shook her head and more pins clattered onto her shoulders and to the floor. "If I were you I would sit down and start working on the problems. Now." A shake of her head and more pins clanked onto the floor.

I kept looking at her wondering if she'd bothered to look into the mirror that morning. Surely if she had seen so many spots she would've put on more face powder.

"Yes ma'am," I said.

I sat down, no less confused. I took off my glasses and rubbed the bridge of my nose. I looked up at Miss Wagoner. Even though my vision is blurry, I could see that her hair was perfectly arrayed, her face flawless. Quickly I put the glasses back on. The spots reappeared. I took them off, squinted at the board. All I saw was white chalk and math problems. No matter how hard I squinted I couldn't see any numbers in gold. I looked down at my glasses. I put them on and the yellow writing reappeared on the board.

Could these possibly be—the answers? I stared at the board for a long time. I was aware that Miss Wagoner was looking at me since I had not written one thing on my paper. So I wrote the first problem down. it wasn't a hard problem so I was able to figure it out all on my own. I looked up at the gold writing. Yes! That was the answer!

It didn't take me long to copy down all the problems with the answers and the work as I saw it written out for me on the board. I did it quite quickly, too quickly and ended up having to slow myself down, to keep pace with my classmates. But still, I was the second person up there with my very clean piece of paper, not even with any pencil smudges or eraser marks.

By the end of that day I knew that these were a pair of very special eyeglasses. Not only did they help me with my arithmetic problems, but I also got the answers to my spelling words and they helped me with my cursive writing, providing lines for me to outline in my handwriting book.

When it came time to go home, I found I wasn't even afraid to walk the dark path. If the big girls were there, I would stare at them through my glasses and they would run away, little bugs that they were.

Which was precisely what happened.

They were waiting for me. They were three abreast across the path holding hands making a human chain which wouldn't allow me to get through. I could see their intention, but through my glasses I could see how flimsy a wall they were. The Biggest Big Girl was in the middle, and right before my eyes she had shrunk to half her size, a complete and perfect miniature of herself. Her face was contorted into a scowl. To her left the Middle Big Girl, the one who had turned into a witch at school, was crying and trembling. Her bony hand shook as she held onto the hand of the miniature Biggest Big Girl. She was shaking so much that the very ground underneath me quaked.

The Littlest Big Girl had turned into a bug with one impossibly long tentacle, the end of which wound around the hand of the Biggest Big Girl. I realized that I could step right over her and be on my way, but my gaze was locked onto the eyes of the Middle Girl who could not stop crying. She looked frightened, about as frightened as I'd been yesterday. Her teeth chattered, and when they did, the ground trembled. Even the ends of her hair shook. It was as if each individual strand of her witch hair had a life of its own.

"Are you okay?" I asked her.

"What? What? What? F-f-four eyes?" She was stuttering so much that it took her a long time to get her words out.

"Are you scared?" I asked.

"N-no. It's you who should be scared. N-not m-me!" With every word she spoke the ground around her shook a little bit more.

"Come on!" said the miniature Big Girl.

"Yeah! Come on," said the Cockroach. "Let's get her!"

I said, "You seem really scared."

"Sh-shut up!" she finally managed. With her last utterance, the ground shook so much that I tripped, but not hard. I was up and quickly on my feet.

I addressed the Middle Girl. "I used to be scared. Then I got these glasses." I pointed. "I'm not scared anymore."

"Well, you should be!" yelled the miniature Big Girl in her tiny voice. "Come on," she called to the others. "Let's get her books again! She can't talk to us like this!"

When I saw what they were intending, I quickly and easily stepped over the Cockroach and made my way down the path toward home, humming as I did so.

"Hey!" yelled the Cockroach.

"How did she do that?" asked the Big Girl.

When I looked back, the Big Girl was yelling at the other two. The Cockroach was scurrying round and round and the Middle Girl was crying so much that tears fell like rain and were forming a puddle around her feet.

***

I am home now with the cold Big Macs, and you are sleeping. You have forgotten all about wanting this sandwich. And margarine. You're not in bed, but in front of the muted television news. Your head is lolled to one side and your mouth is open.

"He doesn't want it now," I say to Marty.

"I guess not," she says. "I'll put it in the fridge for later."

I sit beside you and look at you, at your eyes, the way your face twitches ever so slightly in sleep.

And I remember more.

***

The following morning, my second day with the glasses, I was standing in the hallway and the Big Girls were around the corner. They didn't see me, but I heard them.

"I don't know what happened to her. She seems bigger."

"And did you see her eyes?"

"She just stared at us and stared at us."

"What I want to know is how did she get past us? We were holding hands really tight."

"It was like she walked right through."

"I didn't even see her do it. Did you?"

"No. It was so strange."

"I'm sort of afraid of her now."

"Yeah."

It took me a little while to realize they were talking about me! Bigger? They were afraid of me? Maybe I *was* bigger. Maybe the glasses made me bigger!

Later, after lunch, I heard someone call my name. I turned. Miss Wagoner was there. She didn't look spotty and askew. She looked normal. Even through the glasses she looked nice. And she was actually smiling at me. She was holding onto a piece of paper that I could see was my arithmetic paper.

"Yes, Miss Wagoner," I said.

"I'm so pleased with you," she told me waving the paper. "You got one hundred percent in this test. You must've worked really hard."

I gulped and nodded. A hundred percent?

"I'm so proud of you. I knew you could do it."

I stood there.

"I knew if you put your mind to it, and really buckled down and studied hard you could do this. This shows me that you're really willing to work hard. And I just want to say that if you ever have any trouble with your numbers again, you can come to me. Any time. I'm really proud of you."

"Thank you, Miss Wagoner." My mouth felt dry.

When she walked away I put my hand up to my eyes. Do I tell her about my glasses? Do I tell anyone?

In all these years, I have not.

***

You are awake now and you are lucid. I have turned the news off. None of all of that matters anyway. You have taken my hand and you are talking. "It's a nice day, isn't it?" you are saying.

I nod. "It is very nice." I wonder what year you are living in now. Do I dare ask? I decide to try. "Do you remember—Dr. Seegam? Do you remember him? The doctor you worked for when you were still in school? In Dr. Peterson's office?"

You stare at me, without speaking. There is something behind your eyes. Are you listening? Can you understand me? "I need to know about Dr. Seegam." I say it more earnestly. "You have to tell me about Dr. Seegam. Please. For Anna's sake."

"You have good, ah, good imaginings."

This is what you always say. "You need to tell me."

You pause for a long time before you say, "Someday."

Someday? I stare at you. This is the most you have ever said about the matter. All of the other times during the years of our marriage, you would say, "I really don't know what you're talking about," or, "I'm sure you have me mixed up with someone else," or "I came to your door that day because you had so much spunk I had to meet you. It wasn't about any magic," or, "you really should write all of this down." But after telling me these things you would always wink at me. This word—someday—is

141

as close as you've ever gotten to telling me the truth about the glasses.

"Someday you'll tell me about Dr. Seegam?" I persist.

You wink at me, a feeble gesture now, but it is still there. "Margarine," you say. "Dr. Margarine."

"Dr. Margarine?" I ask incredulous.

"Not margarine. Like margarine. Margin. Margin. Imagine."

"Imagine?" I ask.

You are brightening. "Yes. Imagine."

We were getting somewhere. Maybe. "Imagine? Imagine what?" I ask.

As suddenly as you brighten, your eyes close. I wait. You are asleep. I sigh and get up and Marty spoons out hamburger casserole for us in the kitchen.

***

Like Dr. Peterson promised, my new glasses were ready in two weeks. When my mother told me we had to take the bus that day to pick them up. I balked and said no. Couldn't we please go tomorrow?

To my surprise my mother sighed and said okay.

One more day. One more day of seeing the rainbows on my way to school. One more day of seeing in intricate detail all of the birds in the sky and little animals on the path through the woods, and being careful not to step on them. One more day of seeing their eyes, even, of listening to them say, "Please don't step on us!" One more evening of watching the fireworks from my bedroom window until I was too tired to stay awake. One more night of thinking about my grandmother and seeing the constellations in the night sky right through my ceiling.

I thought about hiding the glasses, or pretending that I lost them, but then I would remember what the kindly Dr. Seegam had said. Other girls needed them. No, I couldn't steal them.

In two weeks the bullies hadn't bothered me at all. In fact I became friends with the Medium Big Girl. A few days after her crying incident in the woods, she had tentatively approached me at lunch and said, "Do you—do you want to be my friend?"

She looked normal that day. She wasn't crying and she wasn't a witch and the ground wasn't shaking with her trembling.

I didn't particularly want to be her friend, because I thought this might be a trap. Plus, I didn't want to be friends with a bully. I told her this and her eyes welled with tears. I remembered the puddle of tears by her feet, so deep and so wide that little sticks could float on it.

She said, "I don't either. But you don't know what it's like! I have to go along with them because if I don't they'll bully me back!"

When we got to the eye doctor's that last day, I looked around. I didn't see either you or Dr. Seegam. The nurse called me over and I took off my beautiful sea blue glasses and put them on the counter. "Here they are," I said.

She ignored them. "Dr. Peterson will be here soon and he'll bring out your glasses. They're all fixed."

"Thank you," said my mother.

"What about the other doctor?" I asked.

She looked at me. "What other doctor?"

"The other doctor who was here, Dr. Seegam. I went back into his office and he gave me temporary glasses."

"Dr. see who?" the nurse asked.

"Seegam," I said. "Dr. Seegam. That was his name."

By this time Dr. Peterson was approaching me, a big smile on his face and my glasses in his hand, "All fixed up and ready to go," he said. "Now you'll be able to see the board again."

"What about Dr. Seegam?" I asked. "Can I see him again? And the other guy? The one in optometry school? I brought his glasses back. You can tell him."

The nurse and my mother were looking at each other. Dr. Peterson was regarding me. "Are you feeling okay?" he asked me.

I smiled brightly. "I'm doing great! I got a hundred percent on arithmetic!"

"Well, good for you," he said.

"Can you tell Dr. Seegam that? That the glasses he loaned me really helped in arithmetic?"

Dr. Peterson looked at me for a long time before he shook his head slowly. "Sadly, I'm the only doctor who's ever worked here."

"No!" I was insistent. "He was here. In the back room. Where I got those—" And I pointed to the sea blue glasses on the counter.

They weren't there.

"Where did you put them?" I glared at the nurse.

"Where did I put what?"

"I put them right down here. The glasses." I put my hand on the counter. "The blue ones. Right here. Where did you put them? You must have put them somewhere." I looked around at her desk, but didn't see them.

My mother grabbed my hands and told me to be respectful.

I was near tears. "But I got glasses. In a big giant room at the back. I tried them on back there. Down the long hall."

Before they could stop me, I ran through the door which led to the examining rooms. They raced after me, my mother sternly calling my name, calling me to immediately come back. Now! We went past examining room after examining room and then the hall ended. It simply ended. I looked around in dismay. "I don't understand. Where's Dr. Seegam? Where's the room? There was a room back here. The hall was longer than this. There were a million glasses back here. In shelves with dust like gold flakes. And rainbows!"

"Oh for heaven's sake," my mother said. She gripped my shoulders to lead me back to the reception area.

"It's okay," Dr. Peterson said to my mother quietly. "She had that blow to her head. These sorts of things have to be expected."

I was confused. I was afraid. I didn't understand. I didn't understand any of this. I became quiet then, subdued, thinking, trying to figure it all out. I said nothing as we walked back into the reception area. As instructed I sat down at one of the tables. Dr. Peterson adjusted the glasses to my face and held up the mirror. I looked at my reflection. They were Coke bottles again. It was me again, the old me, the one that didn't understand arithmetic, the one that everyone called shrimpy and four eyes. The one that was too short. The one that got bullied. My hair wasn't shimmery gold anymore. It was stringy, dirty blonde.

The magic was gone. All of it.

***

Except that it wasn't. Not all of it. When I went to Miss Wagoner she offered to help me.

The Middle Big Girl who became my friend, stayed my friend and we decided that nobody would bully anyone ever again.

***

A month has passed. You never did eat that Big Mac. Marty ended up throwing out the entire McDonald's bag. I am sitting with you all the time now as you lay in your hospital bed. Three weeks ago you took a turn for the worse and we almost lost you. It was a stroke, they told us. Marty and I have been here round-the-clock. When I have been too weary to keep my eyes open, Marty has stepped in, albeit with strict instructions to come and get me immediately if you start talking.

I've decided to finally take your advice. I am writing all of it down. I sit beside you in the hospital and I am writing frantically in a little notebook that I got at the dollar store a week after your stroke. This morning I have decided to try something a bit different. I will read it to you. As you lie there unresponsive, I read long sections of what I have written, probably in vain, I don't know. I am hoping it will jog some sort of a memory in you. I am afraid we don't have much time.

It's funny, living life, going through the years, raising Marty, working with you in the clinic, having friends, traveling. Time passes, life goes on. There would be times, long stretches where I would forget about the magic. Maybe it really was a bump on the head. Maybe a mild concussion had caused me to imagine all sorts of things that weren't real. And yet—

That blow on the head was the thing that changed my life. I remained friends with the Middle Big Girl. Her name is Molly, and we have been friends down through the years. She was Maid of Honor at our wedding. We lost touch briefly, but now we have reconnected on Facebook. We email at least once a day.

Even Molly doesn't know what really happened. All she knew was that I was different the day after my attack. It was her opinion that I finally decided to stand up for myself. But that's not the case. I never would have been able to do that had I not seen the big girls for what they really were, witches, cockroaches and miniature people with tiny voices who think they're bigger than they are.

Your eyes are open now. I stop in my reading and put my book on my lap.

"What is that you're reading?" Your voice is weak, yet clear.

"What?" I manage.

"That story. So familiar."

I lean forward to hear you better. "It's about us," I say. "About how we met. You remember how we met?"

You nod.

"You told me to write it all down, and I am. I'm writing about Dr. Seegam. I'm writing about the glasses, the blue ones. You shined them with a red cloth and a brown cloth before you gave them to me."

"Brown cloth—" You shake your head slightly

as if trying to jog some long ago memory. "That was for the bullies. I wanted to use the black one, but that one wouldn't have worked. That one was for boy bullies—"

I try to keep my gasp inaudible and lean toward you. Our faces are almost touching. There is an excitement in my chest. I put my hand to my heart to try to quell the rapid beating.

"You remember," I say.

You nod. "Yes."

I am full of questions, but something in me decides to wait.

You close your eyes briefly. "I'm in the hospital, aren't I?"

"Yes, you are."

"I'm dying?"

"We all are," I manage.

"Margarine. Margin. Imagine."

I stare at you.

"I was thinking of the word margarine," you say. "But I know the real word I wanted to tell you."

"Imagine. That's what you said."

You are shaking your head. "Not imagine. The word is magic. That's the word I was trying to think about, trying to say. Magic."

Magic?

"Dr. Magic," you say. "That was his name. Dr. Magic."

Dr. Magic? "What about Dr. Seegam?" I ask. "You worked for Dr. Seegam. You were his assistant."

"That's magic backwards."

"What? I don't understand."

"You never knew how he spelled his name, did you?"

I pick up my pen and doodle in my little book. I write Dr. Seegam's name. I write it backwards. M-a-g-e-e-s. And then I understand. If I spell it slightly differently it would be Cigam. "That's his name? Magic spelled backwards?"

You nod. "Quite clever, isn't it?"

"So, he was magic."

You nod, a smile forming.

"Where's the magic now? Where are all the glasses? What happened to them?"

"They're being used. The magic has been passed down. It is still happening."

"What about Anna?"

"She'll be looked after."

I lean toward you. "What do you mean? What do you mean she'll be looked after? Who's looking after her?"

"Anna is being taken care of. I made sure of that."

"Made sure with who?" I am frantic with my questions now. I cannot ask them quickly enough.

"All of my assistants down through the years. You remember the young students who would come and work for me? I passed it on to them. The magic."

I gasp. "You did?"

You nod.

"But why, why did you never tell me?"

"I couldn't. If too many people know about the magic, it would disappear. But I passed it on. I need for you to know this."

"But what is it? How does it work?"

"It's how you look at people. That's what it is, you know. It's all in how you see people. That's the magic of it. That's all there is. That's really all of it. You saw your tormentors as cockroaches and witches and snarly little people and women with spots on their faces and their slips hanging."

I am dumbfounded. "Magic," I say. "It was true all along."

I am conscious of someone standing behind us. The nurse. You are smiling still, grinning, really. The nurse whispers to me, "I couldn't help but hear what he was talking about, cockroaches and witches. That part of it all, the rambling, the talking about magic. His mind's not right. All we can do now is to make him comfortable I'm afraid. I'm afraid he may go on in this vein. If he does, just humor him."

"I will," I say. "I will just humor him. I will be sure to do that."

Beyond the nurse, your eyes are wide with a smile. And then you wink.

About the Author

Linda Hall spent the early years of her writing career as a journalist and freelance writer. She also worked in the field of adult literacy and wrote curriculum materials for adults reading at basic reading levels. In 1990 Linda decided to do something she'd always dreamed of doing, she began working on her first novel. The book she wrote, *The Josiah Files* was published in 1992.

Since that time she's written seventeen more mystery and suspense novels and many short stories and essays.

Most of her novels have something to do with the sea. Linda grew up in New Jersey and her love of the ocean was born there. When she was a little girl Linda remembers sitting on the shore and watching the waves and contemplating what was beyond. She could do that for hours.

Linda has roots in two countries. In 1971, she married a Canadian who loves the water just as much as she does. They moved to Canada and have lived there ever since. One of the things they enjoy is sailing. In the summer they basically move aboard their 34' sailboat, aptly named - *Mystery*.

Both Linda's husband Rik and Linda have achieved

the rank of Senior Navigator, the highest rank possible in CPS. The U.S. sister organization is the U.S.P.S. Linda's Senior Navigator diploma hangs proudly on her office wall. What this all means is that she knows how to use a sextant and can 'theoretically' find her way home by looking at the stars.

Rik and Linda have two grown children, seven grandchildren and a very spoiled cat.

About the Alexandria Publishing Group

The Alexandria Publishing Group is home to a select group of independent authors who certify that their work meets certain professional and quality standards. With self-publishing becoming more and more present in our technological age, it is very easy for everyone to publish books. The Alexandria Publishing Group strives to present books that are a pleasure to read.

If you want to learn more about the Alexandria Publishing Group, its authors and their books, please visit our website at

http://www.alexandriapublishinggroup.com

From the Alexandria Publishing Group, you might also enjoy:

An *Alexandria Winter* story collection 2012

http://www.amazon.com/dp/B005G7ZLDI

An Alexandria Winter Anthology 2013

http://www.amazon.com/dp/B00GW6T4FI/

For a complete list of all Alexandria Publishing Group works, please visit:

http://alexandriapublishinggroup.com/books-by-our-members/

Other books by Linda Hall:

Whisper Lake Series - Steeple Hill Love Inspired Suspense
Storm Warning
On Thin Ice
Critical Impact

Shadows Series - Steeple Hill Love Inspired Suspense
Shadows in the Mirror
Shadows at the Window
Shadows on the River

Fog Point series
Dark Water
Black Ice

Teri Blake-Addison mysteries
Steal Away
Chat Room

Coast of Maine novels
Margaret's Peace
Island of Refuge
Katheryn's Secret
Sadie's Song

The Canadian Mountie Series
August Gamble
November Veil
April Operation

Connect with Linda Online:

Newsletter
http://writerhall.com/contact-me.html

Website
http://writerhall.com

Facebook
http://www.facebook.com/writerhall

Twitter
@writerhall

Night Watch

Chapter One

I was in the middle of a Jesse dream when Kricket disappeared. It was the best Jesse dream I'd had in a long time, and I wanted to stay in that place forever.

We were sailing. We always sail, the two of us, in Jesse dreams. We were out in the middle of the bay on my old wooden catboat, the one I had before I knew Jesse, before he was such a part of my life. I sold that boat years ago to someone who trailered it to Lake Ontario. But dreams are like that, full of curiosities and strange chronologies, yet somehow making full sense at the time.

The wind was a steady ten knots, the sun warm on our necks. We moved effortlessly on the tops of the waves as if across silk. I leaned back, held the tiller with both hands and pressed my sandaled feet down onto the leeward side. The creaking of the pintles, the whoosh of the water beneath us, and the wind filling the sail were the only sounds. We didn't talk.

We don't talk in Jesse dreams.

Down, almost at water level, Jesse was winching the sail in tighter, tighter, one beat-up boat shoe braced against the bulkhead. I looked with longing at the curve of his bare ankle. I wanted to reach out, trace my fingers along its bone, cradle it against my cheek. It had been so long. Too long. Almost two years gone. Yet, in some ways, it will always be yesterday.

I wanted to call out to him, but have learned not to in Jesse dreams. If he turned to look at me, would I see the face with the sun-ruddied grin? The mussed hair always in need of a cut? Or would he stare at me with cold, unseeing eyes, face streaked with blood? Would it be a stranger's face even, which turned to gaze up at me?

Jesse dreams always hold a sharp edge of terror that leaves me breathless and gasping when I finally claw my way up toward waking. Yet, despite this, I crave them, hunger for them. I will take the horror—all of it—for one moment more with Jesse.

Em?

He was calling to me? He never speaks to me in Jesse dreams. I held my breath and watched the muscles in his forearms as he gripped the lines tightly, barely moving as the boat made its way toward ever-deeper water. He moved his foot, and I saw it on the bottom of the boat, wrinkled, wet, lying there—the postcard. I looked away as fear rose in my throat like bile.

Em? He was tapping at my foot, touching it. Over and over. Tap. Tap. Louder.

I tried to speak, could not.

"EM!"

I blinked, opened my eyes wide, and in an instant came fully awake in the half-light. I scrambled out of my berth, knocking my glasses to the sole as I did so.

"Wha-what?" I bent down, grabbed for them. No, I wasn't on a catboat with my dead husband. I was the delivery captain of *Blue Peace,* a fifty-two-foot luxury sailboat, and we were somewhere out in the Atlantic Ocean en route to Bermuda. It was night, and I was being shaken awake by a crew member. No one wakes a captain unless it's a Mayday-Batten-Down-The-Hatches-All-Hands-On-Deck-9-1-1 emergency.

I put on my glasses, tried to focus. Rob Stikles, one of my three crew members, was standing in front of me, opening and closing his mouth, Adam's apple bobbing. The boat moved unnaturally in the sea swells, and I grasped for a handhold.

"You turned the engine on," I said.

"Yeah, um..."

"The winds die? If you're on watch, Rob, you don't need to wake me up every time you have to turn on the engine. I presume you know how to pull in the sails and turn on the engine—"

"It's—it's—not that..."

"What then?" At eye level, we were exactly the same height.

"It's Kricket."

I sighed. He woke me for Kricket? "What? She forget to take her seasick pills again? Is she puking over the side at"—I glanced at the brass clock affixed to the teak bulkhead—"two thirty in the morning?"

I pulled a gray sweatshirt, one of Jesse's, over the T-shirt and sweats I wear when I sleep on boats. "Let me go talk to her." I moved determinedly into the main salon. Kricket would be there, I was sure, lying on a settee in a fetal position, clutching at her stomach and demanding that we turn this boat around right now—*right now*—and take her home.

Behind the nav station, Joan, my chief navigator, was sleeping soundly, only the tiniest scruff of gray hair peeking out from under her thick woolen Hudson Bay blanket. I switched on one of the overhead lights, and the salon glowed eerie red. To maintain our night vision, we use only red LEDs down below after sunset. The light made Rob's face look ghostly, and it reminded me of tenting trips with my two younger sisters and holding the flashlight under my chin and growling at them, and them screaming and holding on to each other until our parents demanded that we all go back to sleep.

"Where is she, then?" I made my way toward the

stern and to Kricket's aft stateroom.

Rob followed me. "She's not seasick. She's um, she's gone." He wailed this out, face flushed. His hands would not be still. His fingers kept crawling up the sides of his squall jacket like crabs. Joan stirred slightly.

Gone? What did he mean? Gone, as in dead? But, no one dies of being seasick. I pressed my palm into my forehead to get rid of the last remnants of Jesse. "Rob," I said, quietly now and trying to muster a certain amount of command to my voice. "Where is she? Where is Kricket?"

"That's just it. I don't know. Well, not for sure. She's..." He paused. "She's not on the boat." He stopped.

I raced up the companionway and out into the icy air which ripped at once through my sweatshirt. "Where is she?" I looked frantically around me but all I saw was black ocean. "She fell off the boat? Is that what you're saying? How did this happen?" I studied the chart plotter.

"Yes." He was behind me and shivering.

"Did you hit the Man Overboard button?"

"The what?"

"On the GPS." I turned and looked him straight in the eyes. "When you saw she went overboard, did you at least hit the Man Overboard button?" Even though I tried to keep my voice even, it was painfully strident at the end of all my words.

"I don't—No. I thought maybe she went down below. So, I didn't. No." His teeth were actually chattering.

The boat made a sideways lunge as we plunged through a sea swell. I grabbed the edge of the binnacle. Carefully studying our track on the chart plotter, I wrenched the wheel around. We would retrace our track. Maybe, just maybe we would be lucky. Once I had again engaged the autopilot, I raced down through the companionway. Rob followed.

"Joan! Peter!" I yelled. "Man overboard! We need you! We need everyone."

Rob slumped down onto a settee and put his head in his hands. I didn't have time to evaluate whether he was crying or not. I didn't know Rob. My other two crew members, Joan Bush and Peter Mauer, were almost family to me. Joan has always been like my wiser, older aunt. She and her husband, Art, were closer to me than my own family after Jesse died. Peter, cook extraordinaire, is like my hunky little brother. I'd known Peter forever. I first met him when I was in high school and taught sailing as a summer job. He was the brightest and smartest little kid in my class of ten-year-olds. I connected with him again when he was a cook on Windjammer cruises, where I crewed for two summers. He'd gone to chef school for a year, but then dropped out to work on boats. We'd been buddies ever since.

We hadn't needed a fourth crew member, yet Peter asked to have Rob come along. His friend was trying to build up his sailing résumé and needed more blue-water experience, he told me.

Yet, after less than a week on the water, I seriously doubted whether Rob had ever been on any kind of boat before. Something as easy as tying a bowline or a simple clove hitch had him fumbling all his fingers. And why had he not thought of hitting the MOB button? There was something else, too, something I couldn't quite put my finger on. He seemed very familiar to me, like I should know him from some place. And it wasn't a good memory.

On top of that, it was clear that there was no love lost between Peter and Rob.

Then there was Kricket. She was the owner's daughter and had come aboard her father's yacht with great reluctance. I'd been told that her father ruled his family like he ruled his corporations and felt his wild daughter needed a bit of an "outward bound" experience.

"And put her to work," Roy Patterson had told me on the phone. "I'm going to be asking you if she pulled her weight."

That little part of the equation had proved difficult, if not impossible.

"What's going on?" Joan sat up now and ran her fingers through her hair. A few strands of it were sticking up at the back. None of us looked our best this time in the morning.

"Kricket's missing," I said. "Possibly overboard."

"What! How? Was she wearing her PFD?" Joan quickly pulled a long-sleeved shirt over her slim frame. I frowned. We had not yet reached the Gulf Stream, where the water suddenly warmed. If Kricket had gone into the frigid Gulf of Maine water, it would be unlikely she would survive, personal flotation device notwithstanding.

"Yes." This came from Rob.

I turned to face him.

"She was wearing her PFD," he said.

"That's something, anyway," I said.

Peter was by now entering the main cabin in sweats and a Mount Gay Rum T-shirt that showed off his biceps. He ran a hand across his unshaven face.

"What's up?" he asked.

"It's Kricket," I said. "We think she's overboard."

A look passed between Peter and Rob, a look I didn't have time, at this point, to evaluate. I grabbed my yellow squall jacket from the hook at the bottom of the companionway and my PFD, stepped into my sea boots and headed topside. Too much time had passed with no one at the helm. Even on autopilot, a careful eye needed to be kept for stray containers from ships and other floating debris.

Joan followed. The wind on this night held a bitter edge and sliced into my face like a sea urchin's spines. In all directions, the ocean was a molten gray of constant movement. It wasn't white-capping, but the swells were high. It caught at me, as it always does, that here we are, a mere speck of flotsam on a huge indifferent sea. I tugged the hood of my jacket up over my head and pulled the elastic toggles tight under my chin, wishing I'd remembered my wool toque. Next time I went down below, I'd get it, along with my gloves.

I tried to collect my thoughts as I followed our jagged line backtracking on the chart plotter. I increased the RPMs and let out a bit of jib to steady us. I tried to remain calm, but I kept swallowing. My cold hands shook. The boat was pitching and yawing in the waves, and I fought back a flutter of nausea. Even in the calmest of weather, the sea is never still. It moves back and forth and sideways, a motion that experienced sailors get used to. It's called "getting your sea legs." But right now all I was feeling was sick.

"Em," Joan said behind me. "Why don't you and I give this boat a thorough going over? There are lots of places where she could be curled up sleeping, cubbyholes and things. Peter and Rob can watch."

Her idea gave me hope. It would be a good idea to exhaust all possibilities before I called a Mayday.

The opulent interior of this custom-built Morris sailboat included two staterooms with their own heads, plus a crew cabin consisting of two bunk-like berths. There were many places where Kricket could be even now. Joan and I went into her stateroom. Because Kricket was the owner's daughter, she got the best room, the aft cabin with its queen-size bed and private head. As captain on this trip, that room should have been mine, but I took the second-best bed, the one on the forward starboard side.

This was the first time I'd been in her room since we left Canada, and I stood in the doorway. If I didn't know better, I would have thought that someone had come in here and trashed the place. Shirts, jeans, sandals, bikini tops and bottoms, and bottles of this and that hair product and makeup looked as if they had been cast here and there in no particular order. Her phone lay across her unmade bed, its earbuds trailing across the mound of clothes like worms. Her Louis Vuitton suitcase was open and heaped with clothes—scarves, sundresses, tank tops, shorts and more.

I rooted through the pile of clothes on her bed. She wasn't underneath. I opened the door to her private head. This was a girl, I realized, who was not used to having to pick up after herself. A cylindrical bottle of designer shampoo rolled back and forth across the sole in rhythm with the sea. I picked it up and put it in the sink.

A feeling of raw fear began to gnaw at my insides. This was my first captaining job after getting my Coast Guard captain's license, and Kricket had to be okay. She had to be. I promised Roy Patterson that I'd take good care of his daughter. Back out in her stateroom, I opened the door to her hanging locker. This is where most sailors keep jackets, fleeces, woolies and foul-weather gear. Not Kricket. Her locker was hung up with pretty summer dresses. Clearly, she was looking forward to party time in the Caribbean. Without speaking, Joan and I went through all of her cupboards and cubbyholes before we left that room to search through the remainder of the boat.

After we had exhausted every locker, every cubbyhole, every closet, every closed and open space on the entire boat, I, Captain Emmeline Ridge had to concede that the absolute worst had happened. We were out in the middle of the ocean, a day from landfall and Katherine "Kricket" Patterson, the daughter of the very rich owner of this magnificent yacht, who'd given me my first-ever captaining job, had truly gone overboard.

I made my way to the nav station. With shaky fingers, I picked up the mic on the SSB radio.

I said clearly and distinctly and slowly, "Mayday, Mayday, Mayday. This is *Blue Peace, Blue Peace, Blue Peace.* We have a man overboard and missing. Repeat, we have a man overboard and missing. We are at latitude—"

www.ingramcontent.com/pod-product-compliance
Lightning Source LLC
Chambersburg PA
CBHW070925130626
46555CB00001B/283